Missing Dad

Missing Dad

4. Mission

J. Ryan

Matador
9 Priory Business Park,
Wistow Road, Kibworth Beauchamp,
Leicestershire. LE8 0RX
Tel: 0116 279 2299
Email: books@troubador.co.uk
Web: www.troubador.co.uk/matador
Twitter: @matadorbooks

ISBN 978 1789013 368

British Library Cataloguing in Publication Data.
A catalogue record for this book is available from the British Library.

Printed and bound in the UK by TJ International, Padstow, Cornwall
Typeset in 12pt Aldine401 BT by Troubador Publishing Ltd, Leicester, UK

Matador is an imprint of Troubador Publishing Ltd

CHAPTER 1

Thin Air

The tide is out. So far out, that only an ooze of water moves between the muddy banks, three hundred feet below. Screaming gulls swoop along the grey cliffs of the gorge. Not far from where we stand here on the bridge, a lone climber hauls himself slowly upwards, battered by the blustery wind.

Becks slips her hand into mine. 'Are you thinking we shouldn't have come?'

'I'm not sure what I'm thinking anymore.'

'That time you came here to feel closer to him...'

I stare down at the brown banks far below. 'It didn't work then... and it's not working now. What am I going to do, Becks?'

'We're going for a walk. The way you're feeling, this isn't a good place to be.' She steers me off the Clifton suspension bridge and we head onto the Downs. Gusts snatch at Becks' mane of red hair and she pushes the flying strands impatiently off her face. 'You're too much alone, Joe. Why not give the sixth form a go after all?'

'With GCSE's like mine?'

'At least you could re-sit your Maths and English…'

I shake my head and we walk on in silence. The sky gets darker and by the time we reach the top of the Downs, rain is falling like icy needles. I raise my head to the clouds to get it full in the face but it can never sting enough.

Becks huddles into her hoodie. 'How's Jack?'

'Gone to Paris on a school jazz trip. At first, he wasn't sure whether he should…'

'Of course he should.'

'That's what I told him. It's not his fault if he can't remember Dad. I wish I couldn't!'

Becks' arm goes round me. 'I don't think you mean that.'

We're at the edge of the cliff now, looking across at the suspension bridge and down into that endless drop, only the waist-high iron railings in our way. And the rage floods over me again. I smash my fist into the rusty metal, harder and harder until the blood comes.

'Joe, stop! Stop it! What are you doing?' Becks grabs at my hand and now hers are all bloody too. Seeing the fright in her eyes takes the anger away as suddenly as it arrived. My legs go and I hit the ground with a bump. She sits down next to me in the wet grass, her face bright with tears. 'I can't bear to see you like this!'

'You might have to get used to it.'

'No!' She takes my face gently in her hands and makes me look at her. 'I know you're angry with your dad for dying. But don't you think your mum is too? How do you think she must be suffering, after all these years of hoping? And what about your grandad? He's lost the son-in-law he loves. You don't have the monopoly on grief, Joe – or anger!'

Looking into Becks' green eyes I feel my face getting hot with shame. 'D'you get angry about your mum leaving?'

'Of course I do. But I feel worse about the things she used to say to me.'

Very slowly, I wrap Becks in my arms and stroke her damp hair. The rain is easing, the occasional sunbeam struggling out from behind the clouds. Our jeans are soaking wet and cold. Her voice is muffled in my hoodie. 'Promise me you'll never harm yourself again?' I hug her more closely, feeling her heartbeat.

—✺—

In the gathering dusk, I walk Becks home from the station. No lights are on in her house. 'Is your dad ever here?'

'I think he's working shifts. Or else it's the new woman in his life.'

'What about Steve?'

'He's working away this week.'

'D'you want to crash at our place? I don't like you being here on your own.'

'It's alright, really. Anyway, I've got school tomorrow.'

'Is there any food in the place? We could get a takeaway…'

'There should be enough milk for a bowl of cereal…'

'That's not a meal! Come and stay with us – Grandad's been doing all the shopping and cooking lately and there's always food on the table.'

She hugs me. 'I'll text you later so's you know that the bogeyman hasn't got me this time – OK?'

—⁓—

When I get home it's dark. In the kitchen, Grandad is pulling some laundry out of the washing machine. He looks at me closely. 'What happened to your hand?'

I run my fingers under the cold tap. 'I fell over… stupid of me. Is Mum around?'

'She had some supper and then turned in for an early night. She's not sleeping at all well, I'm afraid.'

'She should see a doctor – get something to help.'

'That's what I suggested… but she hates taking pills. Frankly, I think she went back to work too soon.' He stacks the laundry in the basket. 'There's pizza in the oven…'

'I'm not hungry, thanks Grandad.'

'Cup of tea?'

'No thanks. I think I'll just get to bed.'

'Joe.' Grandad's pushed his glasses on top of his bald head. I turn in the doorway, knowing what he's going to say. 'This isn't good for you, out of school and with no plans for your future. At least pop into the Job Centre tomorrow.'

'Who's going to give me a job, Grandad? A no-hoper who messed up all his GCSE's except PE?'

'You could re-take them at Stroud College if you don't want to go into the Sixth Form.'

'I'll think about it.'

Grandad reaches out and puts a hand on my arm. 'Joe, it's desperately hard for all of us with your dad gone. But he above all would have wanted you to move on, to get on with your life.'

And now my hands are shaking with that anger again. 'That's just what I can't do, Grandad. I wish I could!'

Back in my room, I've never felt more lonely. Instinctively, I turn to the photo of Becks and me on the Oblivion ride at Alton Towers. Her red hair is flying and she's grinning with delight. Then my phone goes and I look at her text. 'Remember what you promised. X Becks.'

Slowly, I open the drawer where I keep the cutting tools. Small screwdriver kits from Christmas crackers. Amazing what they give to kids in crackers. I pull back my sleeves and survey the scabs and scars that Becks will hopefully never see before they're healed. Then I drop the screwdrivers in the bin.

—⁂—

Sleep is so hard to come by. In the early hours of

the morning, I'm still staring at the wall. Pulling on my dressing gown, I follow the smell of cigarette smoke downstairs and into the garden. Very faintly in the hedge there's a small rustling, maybe from a tiny bird. The grass is cold and wet with dew on my bare feet. Mum is sat at the picnic table, gazing at the hedge where the rustling is coming from. She doesn't even try to hide the fag. 'I'm sorry, Joe. What a lousy example I am.'

Sitting down next to her, I put my arm round her. 'Mum, you're allowed to.'

'What do you mean, love?'

'Point One, I know you'll quit again and next time it'll be for good. Point Two, you need all the battle kit you can get right now.'

Her voice is very tired. 'It won't ever be over, will it? This… missing him…?'

'Monsieur told me that the pain never gets less but you learn to deal with it.'

She looks at me in surprise. 'How would he know?'

I take a deep breath, hoping that Monsieur would want me to tell Mum if it might just help. 'His wife was murdered, not long after his son Arnaud was born.'

'Dear God, Joe. Who….?'

We seem to be in a place where only the truth will do. It would be wrong not to tell Mum about something that has cast such a huge shadow over her life. 'You know the letter from Dad that you gave me, Mum? Where he talks about his suspicious and dangerous employer?'

Her face changes and she whispers, 'She killed Christian's wife? And she killed Julius too, didn't she?'

I nod slowly. 'She's dead herself now. Drowned in a storm in the Mediterranean. Dad defied her to try and save me and Becks and Talia.'

Mum's small hand rests on mine for a few seconds. 'It's courageous of you to tell me all this, Joe. And wise not to have told me before the funeral.'

'There's something else, Mum.' I race upstairs and grab Monsieur's letter from my drawer. 'Dad was incredibly brave… look what Monsieur wrote to me about him.'

Throwing the cigarette butt onto the garden, Mum stands and moves nearer to the light from the back door. She's still standing there, hungrily reading, as I slip back into the house and up to my room.

A thin grey light is beginning to show through the curtains when my mobile goes. My heart thumps as I recognise that familiar voice. 'How are you managing, Joe?'

'Not brilliant, Monsieur. But it's so good to hear from you.'

'And your mother?'

'I'm worried she's going to get ill, Monsieur.'

His voice is gentle. 'I'm afraid that the next few months are going to be the darkest time for you both, Joe.'

'I hope you don't mind but I told her who killed Dad and your wife, Monsieur.'

'You were right to, Joe. Not knowing how a loved one has died makes mourning impossible.' His voice becomes brisker. 'Listen, Joe, I feel that a change of scene is nothing short of essential to you and your mother. I have some possessions of Julius – small mementos – which she should have.'

'You mean… you're inviting us to L'Étoile?'

'If you would like to come. And Becks too, naturally.'

It's like a dazzling ray of light suddenly flooding my room.

CHAPTER 2

L'Étoile

As soon as the plane thunders clear of the runway, Mum fixes me with a direct stare. 'Who's paying for this, Joe? It was all a fait accompli when you told me!'

My face feels hot but I'm just so happy that we're going to L'Étoile. 'Mum, it goes back a bit... Monsieur gave me and Becks this wad of money to keep clear of some rather bad men...'

She sighs. 'He did what I should have...'

'Mum, you couldn't possibly... just chill, OK?' I take her hand. 'We've been able to help Monsieur out too, so we're like, mates?'

She hugs me. 'You and Becks are quite remarkable, Joe. Julius would be proud, I know.' She glances out through the porthole as we sail above endless white clouds in a brilliant blue sky.

'When were you last in France, Mum?'

'I was just asking myself that. It must have been when I took you and Jack to visit the Gautiers in Aix – six years ago?'

'And before you married and came to England, where did you live?'

9

'Very near the Gautiers – numéro dix huit, Rue Espariat.'

'So you grew up speaking French because your mum was French and you were all living in France at the time?'

'C'est ça.'

'And…' I'm not sure how to ask this.

Mum looks at me, her brown eyes sympathetic. 'I'm afraid that, unlike your lovely grandad, your grandmother didn't see marriage as terribly permanent, sweetheart. She went off with another man when I was sixteen.'

I look across at Becks and she nods slightly. She was only ten when her parents split.

'So… Grandad told me he was pretty good at German… but it sounds like he was good at French too?'

Mum smiles, relaxing again. 'In my father's occupation, he had to be a fluent linguist.'

'What WAS his occupation, Mum?'

She shrugs vaguely. 'I think… some kind of diplomat? But on a very discreet level. He never talked about it much. Still doesn't.'

Becks and I exchange glances and we're thinking the same thing: Dad wasn't the only secret agent in our family.

—᙮—

Monsieur is waiting at Marseille Marignane airport with the black Bentley Continental. It gives me a slight shock, remembering the last time Becks and I were here with him, after making that terrifying voyage and going on to Paris, not knowing if Talia was still alive. He greets Mum warmly and they both speak French so fast, I can't make out a thing. She sits in front with him, while Becks and I slide into the leather-scented rear compartment.

'D'you think he'll take us riding on the Camargue again?'

'I hope so. By the way, what excuse did you give the school?'

'I just said that my dad was taking me for a week's holiday. Loads of parents do that at this time of year. Except my dad, of course.'

'I like the way you've done your hair – that tuft thing suits you.'

She sighs. 'It's called a chignon, Joe, as a gesture towards being in France. But thanks anyway.' She smoothes her smart two-piece and I wonder how she puts up with me.

—⁓—

It's getting dark as the Bentley slows outside the tall, wrought iron gates. They swing silently open. Becks and I draw in our breath as those magical little cats eyes gleam on either side of the drive at the Bentley's approach. Above us towers the majestic shadow of the Chateau L'Étoile. But instead of the two lonely lights that we saw on our first visit, the whole of the ground floor seems to sparkle. The sound of some kind of symphony drifts out through the open door where tiny Madame de L'Étang stands smiling. Monsieur opens Mum's door for her and gives her his hand as she steps out. She gazes at the sixteen-point star engraved into the wooden door.

'Remember, Mum? It was L'Étoile Fine Wines that gave me my first proper job?'

She and Monsieur flick me ironic smiles, then Monsieur introduces Mum to his aunt, Madame de L'Étang. She speaks in rapid French to Mum and I think it's a graceful combination of welcome and condolence. Then Arnaud bounds down the steps and flings his arms around me. 'Joe, my dear friend, I am so sorry…'

His eyes are bright with tears and I can feel mine stinging again, but I also know that's OK. In France, boys and men may cry. 'Your dad's been fantastic, Arnaud. I know this visit is going to help…'

He puts an arm round Becks and me and we go inside, followed by the grownups. 'Talia has been flown by air ambulance to the hospital in Aix. She has to stay for another few days to get her strength back and for tests, just to make sure all is well.'

'Tests?'

He hesitates, 'They are a little concerned at the time she is taking to make a full recovery, Becks.'

'But an operation on your heart… it *must* take time.'

'We will all visit her tomorrow – it will do her so much good to see you again!'

Looking at Arnaud's bright eyes with their

shades of worry, I wonder if Monsieur has told Talia about her mother's death. But this is no time to ask. Madame ushers us into a dining room rich with wood panelling. On the walls are two pictures that Becks and I saw in the lounge when we first came to L'Étoile. The cheeky face of the child Arnaud grins opposite the portrait of Monsieur and his wife Lisette on their wedding day. Mum goes over to look at it and turns to Monsieur. 'Elle était très belle, Christian.'

He nods and smiles gently, 'Comme ton mari était beau, Nina. If one day you could spare me a photograph, I would dearly love to have Julius looking down at us from these walls.'

I rummage in my wallet. 'Monsieur – look! Do you remember when this was taken?'

His grey eyes look thoughtfully at the picture of him and Dad. 'Why, it must be ten years ago at least. It was on a skiing trip to Courchevel – you can just see the ski lift in the distance. Julius had some leave but could not return home for fear of being tailed.'

Mum says, 'Sadly, that was so often the case. But please, keep the photo.'

'I will make a copy and return it. Now, all of you, be seated. You must be starving.'

During the delicious meal that follows, I steal cautious glances as Mum chats with Monsieur. That pale, wretched look is gone. Now, her eyes are bright and cheeks flushed from the bittersweet emotions of talking about Dad with the man who was once his best friend.

When I get to bed that night I fall straight into the longest, most soothing sleep I've had in weeks. And when morning comes, I wake with a feeling of happiness that Becks and I are under the same roof.

—⁂—

We have a quick breakfast of croissants and coffee, as Arnaud is impatient to get to the hospital. 'You will need your passports; they have tightened security recently.'

Becks checks in her handbag. Feeling uneasy, I ask, 'Why's that?'

'I will explain later – and no mention to Talia, please.' He drives Becks and me in the Merc and soon we're cruising through the leafy streets of Aix-en-Provence. The hospital looks more like a hotel, with well-cut lawns and tropical plants around the driveway. Only the two armed policemen at the entrance strike a warning note. But they seem to know Arnaud and we're waved inside to reception, where Becks and I have to present our passports and sign a register with our names and addresses. Becks whispers, 'Not quite Gloucester Royal, is it?'

'Smells a lot nicer…'

We find Talia reading in the shade of a large plane tree; she's in a pretty blue, summery dress. Arnaud calls to her, 'Chérie, you have some friends – but you must not get up!'

The book is lowered as those vivid blue eyes take us in and a smile brightens Talia's heart-shaped face.

But I feel a stab of worry as I see the dark shadows under her eyes. She makes a move to stand but then remembers and instead waves to us as we run towards her across the grass. 'My dear friends – this is wonderful!'

Becks and I hug her gently. 'They've let you out of bed, then?'

'They say the fresh air is good, Joe...'

Arnaud frowns. 'As long as it is not too hot... shall I get you some water?'

'I have had plenty, but would you all like some? There is a machine...'

Becks sits down on the grass. 'I love your dress – blue really suits you.'

Talia reaches for Becks' hand. 'It is so good to see you again.'

'Are you getting over the operation OK? Was it very painful?'

'It was, at first.' Her voice changes. 'Sometimes, it still is.'

Arnaud bends over her solicitously, strokes the fine blonde hair and kisses her forehead. 'You have been very brave, chérie. But you still need a lot of rest.'

The husky voice is tense. 'That isn't difficult! I *wish* I had more energy. I've had enough of all these tests and drugs and special food and wheelchairs...!' She bursts into tears, her shoulders shaking.

Arnaud puts an arm round her, his eyes haunted. 'We will soon have you at L'Étoile, with Madame's wonderful cooking.'

'I'm being silly… forgive me.' Talia's eyes wander away from Arnaud's and fix on me. Her voice is calmer. 'I am so very sorry about your father, Joe.'

'Thanks – but you mustn't think about that. You have to get better!'

A young, white-coated medic is approaching with a wheelchair. He smiles at us before helping Talia into the chair. 'It is time for your medication, Mademoiselle.'

She looks almost despairingly at him. '*When* can I leave here, please?'

He flicks a glance at Arnaud and back to her. 'It is not long now. Days, not weeks. But you must eat the good food and the medications we give you. Entendu?'

'Capisco.'

Arnaud kisses her again. 'I will be back tomorrow.'

'And we'll see you again very soon – OK?' Becks turns to Arnaud as Talia is taken inside the building. 'She looked terribly tired…'

'It was a huge operation and she is still very frail. She has to have this medication for her heart every day for the next six months.'

As we make our way back to the carpark, Becks says, 'The sooner she comes to L'Étoile, the better. Then you can look after her, Arnaud.'

Getting into the Merc, I see another armed policeman watching us at the exit.

—∞—

The next few days go by at a gallop – literally, when Monsieur and Arnaud take us to the Camargue. As we splash through the marsh, all the thrills and danger of that ride to Les Baux come back to me and Becks. She kicks on Houragon to try and catch up with the flying white tails of the young horses that Monsieur and Mum are riding, and wheels back to join me, out of breath. 'Your mum's a seriously good rider, Joe!'

I stroke the mane of my faithful Soleil, who still seems to know me after our great escape from Les Baux with Arnaud. He gives me a sideways look and sticks his head straight into the grass, nearly dragging me with him. 'She used to take me and Jack to a riding school when we were small but nothing much rubbed off on me. It was Monsieur who taught me.'

'Well, I thought I could ride but I'll never forget how stiff we were.'

We slow down, as a rider holding a trident comes galloping towards us, shoulder length dark hair flying behind him; he raises the trident and whoops. Arnaud shouts, 'Salut le Guardien!' Becks and I haven't seen Michel since the mighty battle in the Corsican mountains that put paid to the gun toting Bertolini.

'Mes amis! Enfin!' Michel jumps off his horse and hauls us, one by one, off our horses, tumbling and laughing with us in the marshy grass.

He eats with us at L'Étoile that night, and the laughter and storytelling go on into the early hours. Tales of the tunnel and the train, then the men with guns in Bertolini's mountain hideaway get bandied around like they're cartoon stories. Mum listens attentively, occasionally throwing slightly horrified glances at Monsieur, who smiles reassuringly back. At home, I'd always been pretty vague about exactly what happened on my adventures with Becks and Monsieur; but as they're all in the past I can't see that it matters much now.

—◊◊◊—

The following morning we're due to go home. At breakfast, Monsieur takes Mum aside in quiet conversation. She nods and smiles then comes over to sit next to me and Becks. 'Monsieur has generously offered to have you two here for a few more days. I have to get back to work but this visit is doing you so much good, Joe…'

Monsieur joins her. 'And your mother has agreed to come back as soon as she can book more holiday.'

'That's really kind of you, Christian…'

Monsieur puts a comforting arm around Mum. 'Do not forget, Nina, that these visits are good for me also. They keep alive the memory of a brave man who meant a great deal to me.'

As I hug Mum before she gets into the Bentley she whispers, 'Thank you, love.'

'I've not done anything, Mum.'

'Oh but you have. It's through your friendship with Christian that I've been given so many precious memories of Julius that I would never otherwise have had.'

CHAPTER 3

Problems in Paradise

At dinner that evening, both Arnaud and Monsieur seem quiet and preoccupied. Becks and I exchange glances. In the end, I can't bear the thought that we might have outstayed our welcome after all. I touch Monsieur's arm. 'Monsieur, it's really good of you to invite us for a few more days but you must have so much to do…'

His grey eyes are sombre. 'Forgive me Joe, I am being a terrible host. Not least because of the reasons why I asked you to stay on.'

'Sorry…?'

'After I have made a phone call, I will explain. In the meantime, the pair of you may enjoy a stroll in the gardens with Arnaud. The weather will soon be turning stormy.'

Becks and I walk with Arnaud through the gathering dusk, past softly splashing fountains with their statues of Greek goddesses and chubby cherubs. The smell of freshly cut grass mingles with blossom; beneath a cherry tree, a large blackbird is tugging hard at a reluctant worm. That music is coming from the house again. 'Is that Palestrina?'

'Tiens, Joe, you should be on Music Mastermind!'

'Nah… it's from when I was researching…'

'Her.' Arnaud's voice is as hard as a blade. We reach a small pond and I stop to gaze at a tiny toad that's sat on a lily pad; such a bright green that it looks like a jewel. 'Don't go any closer, Joe. It is as poisonous as she was.'

Becks stares at the toad. 'How did it get in here?'

'Perhaps it was always here. But the evil that has arrived at L'Étoile is something altogether new and unexpected.'

I pick up a small pebble and chuck it into the water. The toad leaps and disappears. 'What's going on, Arnaud?'

Heavy drops of rain are falling as we hurry back towards the chateau. Arnaud speaks quietly. 'The phone call that my father is making is to the police. It is to confirm that they have placed an armed guard outside Talia's room until further notice.'

'So… those guards that we saw…'

'Were there for Talia, Joe, because we feel she could be in great danger…'

Monsieur is waiting for us in the dining room. The fine china and crystal glassware have been cleared from the table and in their place is what looks like a long, ruby encrusted pendant on a gold chain. Becks says, 'May I, Monsieur?' He nods. She picks it up and turns its flashing red facets in the light. Then she smiles, 'Sweet', and presses the darkest ruby. The USB connector slides out; we're looking at a very pricey memory stick.

Monsieur waves us into our chairs. 'Would you like coffee?' Everyone wants coffee; I think we're all feeling that very clear heads are going to be needed for what's coming. After Madame's tapping feet have disappeared, Monsieur turns to me. 'Joe, I passed on to your mother a number of mementos of your father, all of which I feel confident will give her only pleasure. They included a wedding photograph and photos of you and your brother Jack, which he always carried with him. But this object is, I feel, safer in your hands.' He picks up the memory stick and it flames with light.

'What's on it, Monsieur?'

'It is not mine to search, Joe.'

'Doesn't look like a man's item, does it?'

'My guess is that your father obtained it from the Contessa.'

'So the sooner we take a look, the better.'

'In the light of something that happened last night, yes Joe. I must ask you to forgive me for my ulterior motive in asking you to prolong your stay, but it is essential that the contents of this device are known.'

'Is it connected with Talia, Monsieur?'

'Arnaud and I feel that it may be.'

Arnaud pulls a sheet of A4 from a folder. 'With Talia due to come here, our top priority was to shield her from the vermin who had turned on her mother... there may also be other criminal elements trying to seek her out.'

Becks asks, 'Has something happened at the hospital?'

'Not as yet, and hopefully now the police presence will suffice to protect her. But last night we had a breach of security here.'

Monsieur takes a sip of coffee. 'We have a networked computer system here and naturally we installed a PC for Talia. We also put a filter on her email that diverts anything remotely suspicious to myself and Arnaud.'

'Of course… she's so frail…'

'And so at risk, Becks.' Arnaud pushes the printout towards us. The subject line of the email makes us freeze.

To my beloved daughter.

But this isn't a message from beyond the grave. The text is brief.

Talia, my darling, I am your father and I can prove it. All I wish for is to have you with me where you belong, after everything you suffered at your mother's hands. Soon, I will let you know what you need to do so that we can be reunited.
Your
*   P*

'What does 'P' stand for?'

'It could be short for Padre or Papa, Joe. If this lowlife is trying to make Talia believe who he is…' Arnaud can't keep the anger from his voice.

Becks whispers, 'What kind of sick perv…?'

22

'I thought you said her father was dead, Monsieur.'

Monsieur frowns as he looks at the email. 'It was thought that the Contessa did away with him, but there was no conclusive evidence. The most alarming aspect is how this person knew that Talia would be coming here, and how he managed to hack into our network to try and get this email to her.'

In my mind, I'm seeing those deadly rockets as they soared over the Contessa's Merc, nearly killing Monsieur and Becks and me on the way to Marseille. 'You think that it could be someone from her gang, Monsieur?'

'We cannot be certain. She had many enemies. We need more information... '

I pick up the memory stick; it flashes furiously in the light from the chandeliers. 'Do you think Dad took it from her, Monsieur, or...'

'It is possible that she gave it to him as some kind of thank you. Your father was exceptionally good at his cover job.'

'So we've got to find out if it can tell us anything about this husband and how he disappeared.'

—◊—

We all gather round Arnaud's laptop as he inserts the glittering memory stick. As soon as it opens a window pops up, demanding a code. 'Let me, Arnaud – this might work.' Monsieur's fingers fly across the keyboard and we're in. 'If Julius used this stick to communicate with his agents, we need to look for a folder named Uploads. Ah – here it is.' He double clicks and the folder opens.

'Uploads? You mean he used, like, a wiki?'

He nods at Becks. 'Which one could only access using a codename.'

'Like Icebreaker, or Le Loup?'

'Correct again.'

'Was that your codename you used to access the stick?'

'There was a chance that it would work…'

'What was my father's codename, Monsieur? He mentioned the three musketeers in a letter to Mum. 'Tous pour un, un pour tous…''

His grey eyes study mine. 'I think you can guess, Joe.'

'Was it D'Artagnan?'

He smiles. 'So you will not be surprised to know that my codename was Aramis. Now… you and Becks have some reading to do.'

'Don't you want to go through it with us?'

'The memory stick is now yours, Joe. It is better that you look at your father's messages before sharing them.'

'But there could also be stuff that she put there…?'

'Very possibly. And of course I will look at that with you.'

—m—

We stare at the maze of files in the Uploads folder. 'God, Becks, where do we start?'

'Let's see if we can get at dates.' She clicks on Details but only the file sizes are revealed. 'He must have put some protection on it, in addition to the password.'

'Then we'll just have to go for it. What about this one?' I click on the file named *I made first contact....* and suddenly we're inhabiting the dangerous world where Commander Julius Grayling once worked.

Mes chers amis

I made first contact with Milady de Winter today. She bought my story that I am seeking new employment since the Black Knight became a guest of Her Majesty. She told me that her former bodyguard had met with a misfortune (I know he did – the misfortune was me), and so she may well be interested in my services. My SAS experience counted in my favour, as did my work with the Black Knight (little does she know that I was instrumental in his change of circumstances). I am to return tomorrow to discuss terms. I don't doubt that in the meantime she will thoroughly check me out.

Amitiés à tous
D'Artagnan

'Your dad was in the SAS? Awesome.'

'He mentioned it in a letter Mum showed me. But who's this Milady de Winter?'

Becks chews at a lock of red hair. 'It must be

another code name, like the Black Knight. I think she was in the Dumas novel...'

'I bet Monsieur and Arnaud would know – and they've probably got the novel, anyway.' I search through the bookshelves while Becks goes to look for Arnaud. Just as I find a vintage, leather-bound copy of *Les Trois Mousqetaires*, Arnaud and Becks hurry into the room.

'She was horrible, Joe! She poisoned people...'

Feeling sick at heart, I put the book on the dining table. 'So she's the Contessa. Becks... I'm not sure I can do this...'

'Joe, I know it's hard, but we could find out something about this perv who's posing as Talia's father...'

Behind my rushing thoughts, Dad's voice chimes quietly in my mind. I hadn't expected to hear his voice ever again. I sit down with the laptop. 'Where do we go?'

Arnaud points. 'What about that one? An amusing incident...'

Salut les mousquetaires!
An amusing incident just prior to my second meeting with Milady de Winter. She had, it would seem, decided to obtain firsthand knowledge of my capabilities, but it was ineptly done. One of her henchmen made a clumsy attempt to take me out by her swimming pool. Unfortunately for him, I glimpsed his reflection in the water as he lined me up in his sights. Despatching him was like

26

taking candy from un enfant. I left him enjoying a relaxing swim, face down. This little scene decided me to negotiate double the rate of pay that I had first considered. She did not hesitate. In fact, I caught the faintest trace of respect in her froideur. I start tomorrow. There will occasionally be chauffeuring duties, but as she has an excellent taste in exotic machines, I imagine this will be quite entertaining.

Votre
D'Artagnan

Arnaud says quietly, 'Your dad must have been a crack shot, Joe.'

'He writes about it all so casually, yet it's life and death…'

'I think he was not afraid of anything, Joe.'

'Well, your dad took on Bertolini and called his bluff, didn't he?'

'There's one here that refers to a gift.' Becks clicks on a file.

Chers amis
An unexpected gift from Milady today, in addition to the pay rise after the incident with the sniper. Duly reconnaissante of my efforts on her behalf, she presented me with a pretty ruby trinket with a mind of its own, which she said had belonged to her late husband. Despite finding this privately a somewhat morbid token, I felt it would be rash to enquire how the gentleman departed this life, and accepted the gift graciously.

Becks looks at the flashing gems of the memory stick. 'A ruby trinket with a mind of its own…?'

My mind's racing. 'Do you think there could be stuff from her late husband on the stick?'

Arnaud shakes his head. 'She'd have wiped it, surely? She must just have given it to your father for the value of the rubies.'

'So there's probably nothing of hers on there either. She'd have deleted everything.'

Becks yawns. 'There's delete and there's delete… but can we go on with this tomorrow? I'm shattered.'

Arnaud takes out the memory stick and hands it to me. 'Your father worked in a deadly world, Joe.'

'If only he'd had a boring job, he'd still be alive.'

'He was not that kind of man – and neither are you.'

—๛—

That night, I dream for the first time in weeks and I don't enjoy it. I'm in a churchyard, at night, and there's this thumping. Then I realise that there's an open grave right in front of me and someone's banging on the coffin lid. I watch, horrified, as the lid starts to lift and then I wake up. Arnaud's knocking on my bedroom door. 'Joe, there's been another email!'

'And the Contessa could have been lying when she told Dad her husband was dead!'

We all meet up in the dining room and Monsieur hands me the latest. His face is severe.

Dearest Talia

I need a sign from you that you wish to join me. I repeat, I can prove that I am your father and will explain why I had to flee your mother. Once you are with me, I will be able to ensure that you lack for nothing. Simply click on Reply and send me the one word I long to have from you – Father.

Your loving

P

Arnaud stares at the email and whispers, 'I would like to ram it down his perverted gullet!'

I pour us all coffees. 'He's given rather a lot away in this one, don't you think?'

Monsieur's grey eyes fix mine. 'I knew that you would be able to take the more objective view that we need, Joe.'

Breakfast is served, with Madame de L'Étang clucking at the maid like a mother hen; then we're left in private. I take a gulp of café au lait and read from the email. '*Once you are with me, I will be able to ensure that you lack for nothing.* Sounds to me like this dude is broke right now and wants to get at money that Talia could inherit.'

Becks frowns. 'I thought the state was going to confiscate all the Contessa's wealth, Monsieur.'

'That is what the chief prosecutor told me. But this person might know of an inheritance from another source.'

For some reason, everyone looks at me. 'Yeah, well, could it be pointing to this low life being a cheap fraud – and Talia's real dad maybe having saved up some money for her?'

Arnaud exchanges a look with his father. 'I think you have it, Joe! If this man was genuine, he would approach through the official route and not trade on a fragile young girl's emotions.'

'Trouble is we still don't know if Talia's real dad is dead or alive.'

'The memory stick must have more to yield, Joe.' Arnaud pushes cups and plates out of the way and opens his laptop. I take the shimmering red stick on its gold chain from round my neck, where I've been wearing it like a talisman. Arnaud continues, 'I am going into the hospital to see Talia and check that the police guard is discreet, as they have been instructed. We don't want her to know anything about this until it's been resolved. Maybe not ever.'

Monsieur puts down his half full coffee cup. 'In the meantime, Becks, I would like to draw on your talents to see if we can track down the person who has invaded L'Étoile in such a sinister way. I am reliably informed that you are quite a technocrat?'

'What have you been saying, Joe?'

'Only that if anyone can track down where these emails are coming from, you can. Oww!' It's really painful when Becks kicks my ankle wearing heels.

Smoothing the chignon, she stands up in mock indignation. 'His confidence is touching, Monsieur. Now, take me to your computer.'

―⁂―

Madame de L'Étang supervises the clearing away of a breakfast that's barely been nibbled at and then I'm left to myself. I enter 'Aramis' to get in and go back to the Uploads file. It's strange, trawling this dark world that Dad had infiltrated. An odd sort of file name catches my eye – *A mission for Michelangelo*. I click it open.

Greetings from the Shades
Milady talks seldom about her daughter, who is being educated at a private school in Geneva (Dieu merci, with a mother like this one!). However, with my ear to the ground, I am picking up rumours, probably apocryphal, that there was a twin brother. Word has it that the father, realising what a fury she is, snatched the boy child immediately after the birth, but was unable to save the girl. Mes amis, if any of you can enlighten me on this, the information could be most useful to us one day. Michelangelo, I believe you have more knowledge of Milady's activities at that time than any of us. I would be most grateful for any nuggets you can provide.

Veuillez agréér, messieurs, mes sentiments sincères

Votre

D

For a few minutes, I stare at Dad's nonchalant words like I've had an electric shock. Then I race into the lounge. Becks and Monsieur look up from the computer in surprise. 'You'd better come and look at this – quick!'

Monsieur scrolls back and forth through the message. 'This must have been sent after I had to leave the network. I never met the agent Michelangelo, but I gather he was Oxford educated like Julius and spoke very good Italian, with extensive local knowledge in that part of the underworld.'

'It's problematic, isn't it?' Becks pushes a stray lock of hair behind her ear. 'The hacker's saying he's the dad who apparently fled from the Contessa... which could be the case.'

'I can't buy that. He never mentions any son; I still think he's a fraud.'

Becks nods at me. 'Plus, like Joe says, if the real dad cared enough about his kids to try and rescue them from her, he could also have set up some kind of inheritance for them.'

Monsieur says thoughtfully, 'If the son was a twin he would be seventeen now, like Talia.'

'D'you think he's still with his father, Monsieur?'

'That depends on whether the father evaded her. The Contessa reached out from the past to many more than me.'

Those cold hands are on my neck again, as I remember the dreadful fury for vengeance that died only when she did. 'Monsieur, could you get in touch with Michelangelo? I mean, we've got to do something.'

'You are right, Joe; there could be more lives

than Talia's at stake now. I may be able to trace him through some agents who are better known to me.'

'Did you have any luck with the hacker, Becks?'

'I think he was using a different internet café each time he emailed. But hacking is an offence and the police can force the Internet Service Provider to disclose who the emails are coming from.'

Monsieur picks up the landline. 'We must move quickly. I don't like to think what this man may do next.'

'Are you talking about our pet rat?' Arnaud makes us all jump as he comes in swiftly and silently through the open French windows. Monsieur explains about Dad's message. Arnaud's face is incredulous. 'Talia could have a *brother*?'

'We have only hearsay, Arnaud, but it is obviously imperative that we try to find out.'

'The more so in the light of my visit to Talia this afternoon.' Arnaud sits down at the table with us. 'Talia asked me about her mother. I… told her what happened on the Lisette.'

Monsieur frowns. 'It was a risk, Arnaud.'

The ruby stick flashes fire as Arnaud picks it up and turns it in the light. 'Talia knows more than we thought about her mother. She regarded her only with fear.'

Becks watches the glittering gems. 'That's very sad… if only we could find her brother… if there really is a brother….'

Arnaud carefully replaces the memory stick. 'In

the meantime, we have a great deal to do in a short time, Father. Talia is being discharged at midday tomorrow. L'Étoile must be made as safe as a fortress for her.'

CHAPTER 4

Eyes of the Night

That night, I can't sleep at all. It's like the night after we buried Dad. All I could hear was this silence that wasn't his voice; all I could feel was this space in my head where he wasn't. In the end I give up trying, get up and go to the window of my bedroom.

The chateau has tall windows, each with many panes, some of them made of stained glass that casts rainbow shadows. In my room, the window goes from the floor almost to the high ceiling and it forms a double door onto a balcony. And tonight, the moon is so bright that a path of multi-coloured light shines all the way across my bedroom floor. As I open the double doors, the scent of lavender from the gardens below washes over me. I can hear the whispering fountain. The iron rail of the balcony is cool on my hands. It reminds me of the time when I was a small kid, gazing down through the railings of the Clifton suspension bridge over the river Avon at full tide, my hand in my father's. Looking at Monsieur, as he motored his beautiful yacht gently up the river.

Staring down into the gardens I can see no lights;

the cats' eyes on the drive only come on when there's a car. But I can hear something. It sounds like a low scream, going 'Aah, Aah!' in the distance through the trees and it makes me shiver. Gripping the rail harder, I listen for it again.

'Joe!' Becks' hissed whisper makes me jump a mile high. 'Joe?' She's on the balcony next to mine, craning to listen like I am.

'Yeah, I know. What's going on?'

'See you by the fountain. And for God's sake, be quiet!'

Creeping down the stairs, I'm uncomfortably aware of what could happen if we set off a burglar alarm or some other security alert. Monsieur and Arnaud are worried enough about Talia, even with her hospital police guard. And I have no idea what security systems are in place here at L'Étoile.

Becks is waiting for me in her shorts and top. The night air is warm with the gentlest of breezes. The softly splashing water from the fountain mingles with the sawing string notes of crickets. 'What did you hear, Becks?'

'Some kind of scream or cry – not sure if it's a human or an animal. I haven't ruled out vampires or werewolves, of course….'

I take her hand. 'I think they're all a bit passé in France. But we might as well take a quiet stroll to check it out.'

We step warily between clouds of buzzing mosquitoes and enter a wide avenue where giant trees spread their branches like layers of fans. Becks twirls a lock of hair between finger and thumb. 'What d'you think about this creep, Joe?'

'I don't think he's Talia's dad.'

'No – but he could be a leftover from the Contessa's gang. Remember the car that followed us on the way to Marseille… ?'

'Someone must have ordered them to get her car… but did he know we were in it? Or did he think it was her?'

'He couldn't have known it was us.' Becks watches as a small orange moth alights on her hand. She keeps her hand very still as the moth flares its wings, revealing their elaborate, frilled beauty. She whispers, 'I think the leftover's still around, pretending to be Talia's father. We need to revisit the ruby stick.' She moves her hand gently and the pretty moth flies into the night.

That cry comes again. 'Aagh!'

'For God's sake what IS that?'

The cry seems to come from above. We're near the towering wall that surrounds the chateau, lit by built-in lanterns. We look up, but all I can see is darkness above the ancient stones. Then there's a brief flapping of powerful wings and all is quiet.

A second later, all the lights in the chateau come on and we can hear shouting. I grab Becks' hand and we run for the French doors. As we stumble into the lights of the dining room, Arnaud's face is blazing with anger. 'They have abducted her from the hospital!'

Monsieur is on the phone to the chief of

Marseille police. Arnaud speaks quietly, 'It seems they got in through the roof and badly beat up the two policemen who were guarding her.'

'Do they know who it was?'

'No. Dear God, this could kill her even if the shock and fear don't – she needs the medication daily!'

'Could it be the perv who was emailing her…?'

'When he found out her real whereabouts… could be but we don't know anything, Joe!'

'Or could it be the people who followed us when we were in the Contessa's car?'

Monsieur puts down the phone. 'It is very possible that these are her men.'

Becks sits slowly. 'Oh God…'

'And I, who undertook to shelter her, have allowed this horror to happen…' Monsieur's voice holds an anger that I've seldom heard as he stabs another number into the phone pad.

I sit down and take the ruby memory stick from around my neck where it's beginning to weigh like the Ring of Power. 'I think there could be something here… something I've missed.' As Arnaud opens up his laptop I stare at the glittering crimson stick.

'So you want to trawl the rest of the stick?'

'I have to, Arnaud. And it has to be now.'

Becks sits down next to me. 'Not without me you don't. You'll fall asleep.'

—◊—

Monsieur has sent in trays of coffee, juice and biscuits and he's on his mobile in the next room. My head is starting to ache when I get this lightning strike. 'Michelangelo – I'm sure he can tell us more, Becks.'

'He was the one your dad was going to contact about the twin brother, wasn't he?'

'Do we know if Monsieur has made any progress in tracking him down yet?'

'I'm sure he'd have said, but…' Becks runs next door.

Monsieur comes back in with her, shaking his head. 'I have made contact with Icebreaker and The Highwayman. They say they haven't heard from Michelangelo in years.' Looking exhausted, he sits down in an armchair by the stone fireplace.

'What about Zeitgeist? He sent a bouquet to Dad's memorial too, didn't he?'

Monsieur stares into the stone fireplace. 'Zeitgeist has disappeared with no trace.'

Becks comes to sit down quietly on the floor in between us. 'Things are going wrong in the network aren't they, Monsieur?'

He murmurs, 'So it would seem.'

'Have you tried Le Loup, Monsieur? He sent a bouquet for Dad as well, remember?'

'I am waiting for him to get back to me. It is possible that he has information that could help.'

As Monsieur leaves the room, I whisper to Becks, 'There was no bouquet for Dad from Michelangelo, was there?' She shakes her head.

We do a search of all the directories that we can find in the ruby memory stick and there is no more Michelangelo. So then we search under Palestrina Boy Twin, Palestrina Girl Twin and turn up nothing.

—⁓—

Becks rubs her eyes. It's three in the morning. 'So now it's wild card time. Try 'Talia'.' The internal search engine of the memory stick doesn't give us a chance to enter 'Talia'. As soon as we key in the 'T', it flags up 'Traitor'. And a whole new folder appears that we never knew was there. I click on it and open the Word document. It contains three names. Becks frowns. 'Sebastian. Who's he?'

'No idea. As for Michelangelo, he was part of the network. Now, Dad has him down as a traitor. And there's this Amadeo. What was going on?'

'Who did he share it with?'

I click on Uploads and scan the files. 'It's not here.Maybe he didn't share it with anyone.' Then, I have an idea. 'What do you do if you think that someone you're sharing information with is sending it to the enemy, Becks?'

She slowly sips her café au lait. 'You mean, if you don't trust anyone at all in the network?'

'That's the difficult one. Surely Dad had someone he could trust.'

'Like Monsieur?'

'Yeah – exactly.'

Becks frowns. 'But suppose all this happened after Monsieur had to leave the network?'

'I hadn't thought of that.'

'But surely all those agents who sent flowers to your dad's memorial must have been his friends? People he could trust?'

'You'd think so, wouldn't you?' My eyes ache. Faint traces of a grey dawn are tinting the horizon. I get up and steer Becks through the French windows and into the scented garden. The grass is soft under our feet as we walk, her hand in mine. 'Might he have emailed the other agents to warn them about Michelangelo?'

'Not secure enough.'

'How would you have done it, Becks?'

'I suppose one way could have been to block Michelangelo's password while the warning went out to the other agents...'

'But that would have made him suspicious, wouldn't it?'

'And that could be no bad thing. Another way could be to simply announce that someone in the network is a mole and see what kind of responses that triggers.'

'That could be a bit horrific, couldn't it? I mean, the whole network is based on trust.'

Becks shakes her head. 'Trust can be blind. An organisation like the network has to be based on intelligence supported by evidence, first and last.'

'God, Becks, you sound like M!'

Becks twirls a strand of hair. 'I think, one day, I'd like to be M.'

'What, film star M or actually head of MI6?

'Head, of course! Loads of women are in that kind of top job now.'

'Who d'you think Michelangelo was feeding information to?'

'Suppose it's someone who even the Contessa feared – you know, like Bertolini was terrified of her? We're not finished with the ruby stick yet, are we?'

'Damn – I should have taken it out of the laptop.'

Becks tries to sound reassuring as we race back towards the chateau across the damp lawns. 'We've only been away a few minutes…'

But the ruby memory stick is gone. A frantic search reveals nothing. Everything else is untouched. Becks' cold coffee. All the papers around the laptop. The laptop itself, still powered up. Becks stares. 'Some bird has crapped on my chair!' And I wish I had a gun that could bring down whoever took the one precious link I still shared with my dad.

—∞—

'You should have backed it up, Joe!' Arnaud's voice shakes with anger.

My face is hot. 'I know.'

'This was so foreseeable!'

Monsieur touches his son's arm. 'Gently, Arnaud. Nothing that has happened in the last twenty four hours has been in the smallest way foreseeable.'

I glance up at the movement detector in one of the top corners of the room. 'I guess, while we've all been still up, the alarms were off, Monsieur?'

'Only inside the chateau. There are sensors that will catch any attempt to climb the walls.'

Becks mutters, 'But not fly from the walls…'

'We found out something that could give us a clue, Monsieur.' I grab a sheet of notepaper and scribble down the three names. 'Dad had a file called 'Traitors'. These names were in it.'

His face changes as he reads. 'Sebastian – I know nothing of this name. Michelangelo… is hard to understand. This agent had been in the network for years…'

'Who was Amadeo, Monsieur?'

He sits and pours himself a café noir. 'Not 'was', Joe, unfortunately. He is still very much alive. As the late Contessa's second-in-command, this man had a lust for power that matched her own, but not her intelligence.'

'Did he send the car with the rocket propelled grenades?'

'It could only have been him. But he must have thought his men were aiming at her, in her moment of weakness.'

'D'you think this Amadeo is the guy posing as dad? Or is he behind Talia's abduction?'

'It could be both'. Monsieur puts down the café noir and stands. 'I am going to Avignon to see Le Loup. He is the only agent in the network who might be able to help.'

'We are going together, Father! I will bring the Merc round.' Arnaud disappears at a run.

'What can me and Becks do, Monsieur?'

Monsieur pauses at the door and looks at us. 'You must wait here with Becks – these men are deadly, Joe.'

As the door closes behind him, Becks sits down at Arnaud's laptop and types 'Palestrina' into Google.

'What are you looking for?'

'Someone beginning with M.'

'Do you think Michelangelo was somehow tied up with her?'

'If your dad had him down as a traitor it could have been her he was in with, couldn't it?' She hits Enter and the same website pops up as when we were researching the Contessa.

'No change there then…'

But Becks stares intently. 'It's a place, isn't it? An ancient city not far from Rome – suppose the father has snatched her and this is his home town?'

'You mean the father's called Palestrina? I always thought that was like, all part of the Contessa's title?'

Becks rubs her eyes. 'Whatever – I still think they could be linked, don't you?'

'I suppose…. God, if only we still had the memory stick!'

We both jump as that 'Aagh!' echoes again out in the garden. It seems nearer than before.

—◊—

Dawn slowly filters a pale gold light through the curtains as we trawl the net for anything that could give us a clue about where they've taken Talia. At last, my eyes just won't stay open; I must have fallen into a half doze when Becks hisses, 'What's that noise?'

'What...?'

'Listen...'

We wait, not breathing. Then it comes. A scratching on the glass of the French windows. 'It sounds like some kind of animal...'

'Let's find out, shall we?' Becks strides across to the doors and throws them open, pulling back the curtains. We stare out at the garden with its softly murmuring fountains; sunlight glints faintly on the falling water. Becks steps outside and looks around. 'I can't see anything...'

As my arms are wrenched behind my back, I can't help shouting out with surprise. Then I shut up; the knife is far too close to my throat. 'You move an' this does!' Cold and sharp, the knife touches my neck.

At the same moment Becks says quietly. 'Let go of him.' Slowly, she starts to advance into the room.

My captor hisses, 'You move, he gets this.' Trying to make out who has me in this grip, I test his hold very slightly. The knife nicks my throat. 'You can' hear?'

There's a blur to my left and suddenly the knife is flying through the air. The stranger releases me and lunges for it. The whirling dervish kicks him in the chest and he falls. Struggling to his feet, gasping for breath, he throws himself across the floor after the knife. But Becks gets to the blade before him and now she's holding it close to his neck as he sprawls on the floor. He's about our age but so thin he's way more bone than muscle. Dark bruises show on his arms, and there's an open sore on his forehead. His jeans and shirt are ragged and filthy, like he's not looked after by anyone. The greasy hair is blond and the red-rimmed eyes could be blue.

Becks says quietly, 'We really don't want to hurt you. But we really don't want you to hurt us. Deal?'

He nods, like he's so tired he's run out of words. I put an arm beneath his shoulders and help him to a chair. 'You hungry?' He nods again. Becks gets some coffee from the machine in the kitchen and brings a plate of biscuits. He devours them like a starving animal, and gulps the café au lait. I whisper to Becks, 'Where did you learn to fight like that?'

She looks at me strangely. 'You know Lenny's been teaching me kick boxing.'

'Oh, right.'

'I'm going to get him some milk. Too much coffee isn't a good idea.' Becks disappears into the kitchen again. The boy keeps on wolfing those biscuits like he can never get enough. When Becks comes back with the glass of milk, he gulps it down so fast I hope he's not going to be ill. Then he stops eating. He's looking at us; and behind the tiredness in his eyes is a huge question.

Becks says softly, 'I'm Becks Bowman and this is Joe St. Aubin. Do you want to tell us your name?'

The boy wipes his mouth with his sleeve. He looks at me and shakes his head. 'Your name… not St Aubin.' I can hear an accent but it's not French. Maybe Italian. And his voice sounds so familiar. The blue eyes bore into mine and I've seen them before.

'What makes you think that?'

The boy's head rolls to one side in exhaustion. Becks says quickly, 'You don't have to tell us right now. Would you like somewhere to sleep?'

With a huge effort he pulls himself upright and the blue eyes blaze at us. 'There is no time to sleep. I have to find my sister an' you must help me!'

There's a silence in the room as more pale light floods in. It glints on the boy's golden hair, so like the colour of hair that we last saw only a few days ago. Gently, Becks takes his hand. 'You're Talia's twin brother, aren't you? What's your name?'

Sweat on his forehead, the boy whispers, 'My name is Tommaso. Will you help me?'

Becks says, 'You look like you need to sleep, Tommaso. And maybe we get you a doctor?'

'No!' Tommaso struggles to his feet, his voice surprisingly powerful. 'We must go now! I know where they've taken Talia…'

'You know where they've taken her? How?'

He turns to me, blue eyes with dark shadows beneath them. 'I will tell you on the way. You can drive, Joe Grayling, can' you?'

Shocked at his use of my real name, I stare at this skinny, bruised boy who is Talia's brother. 'How do you know so much about me, Tommaso?'

Impatiently, he throws me a car key. 'I have had plenty of time, Joe Grayling.'

Catching it, I recognise the Bentley key. 'Where did you get this?'

'Oh, that… ' Tommaso gives a low bird call that reminds me of how Michel called the horses on the Camargue. On wings that flare like fingers, long tail balancing, the raven cruises effortlessly into the lounge through the open French windows and lands casually on the back of an armchair. In the light from the chandeliers, his plumage glows with dark silken blue and black. His bright black eyes view us with contempt mixed with a degree of friendliness. Tommaso strokes the bird and it raises a sharp beak towards him, chattering quietly. 'This is Corbo. He likes bright things. But he'll give yours back if you can help us.'

Becks says, 'Actually, Tommaso, that memory stick may be able to help you and Talia just as much as us.'

Tommaso whispers to Corbo, running a light hand over the dark, feathered body. With a clatter of wings, Corbo takes off, disappears outside for a few seconds and then drops gracefully into Becks' lap, depositing the memory stick. He takes off again, lands on the chandelier and watches us, head on one side, curved beak gleaming.

'Thanks, Corbo.' Becks drapes the golden chain

round her neck. Corbo does his blood curdling 'Aagh!' and lands on the floor by the knife.

Very slowly, Tommaso walks across to where the knife is lying on the floor, stoops and picks it up. 'I cannot be without this. But I promise you that I will only use it to protect myself and you, my friends. Now, can we go, please?'

'Give me half a sec – I need to get some cash.'

'You may also need your passports.'

Becks and I keep a watchful eye out for Madame de L'Étang as we creep out to where the Bentley stands in the drive. Once we're inside the leather-scented interior, I hesitate. Here I go again, back to my mad, bad and dangerous driving days and all the fear of getting caught and locked up. We've not had the dosh for me to take my test. And this isn't my car. 'Shouldn't we at least contact Monsieur… in case…?'

Instantly, I can sense Tommaso tensing up in the front passenger seat. From the back seat, Becks' voice is not what you argue with: 'Joe, I honestly think that we've got far more chance of finding Talia than Monsieur has right now and I'm sure he'd agree – we have to go!'

I start the engine and the mighty Bentley whispers into life. 'Over to you, Tommaso. Somehow I don't think this is a job for sat nav…'

Becks hisses, 'Definitely not – sat nav can't be programmed to look out for cops.'

'Or the Camorra.' Tommaso speaks so quietly that I can't be sure I've made out the words. Was it Tomorrow? What does any of us know about Tomorrow?

CHAPTER 5

Tommaso

No one talks during the first part of the journey. I have to work hard to get to know the Bentley controls because they're different from the one I drove for Monsieur in England; this car is left hand drive and it's only the second time I've driven a left hander. It's like you have to re-train your hands and feet. Then there's the familiar terror of getting caught. Every time I see just a harmless cyclist my hands go clammy. By the time we reach Marseille, the sun is blazing in a clear blue sky and I'm feeling about as inconspicuous as a live pig in a slaughterhouse. Tommaso reels off road numbers until my head spins.

'Like, where are we headed?'

'Italy.'

'That's quite a hike, isn't it?'

'Where we are going is just over a thousand kilometres from Marseille.'

'Right…'

'Is Corbo flying all the way?'

Tommaso shakes his head at Becks in the mirror.

'No. The crow family are not so good over long distances. He will be travelling the same way we came. By train and truck.'

'What...?'

'We hitched lifts in cattle trains and lorries. Is the safest way.'

I nod, storing this in my limited memory pack. 'Yeah. Course it is.'

The French part of the drive is pure James Bond country, with the Bentley gripping like a python along twisting coast roads above a sea of deepest blue. I keep catching Becks' reflection in the rear view mirror; green eyes bright, red hair floating in a sort of cloud, she's gazing down at a tiny white-sailed yacht far below. And despite the fear for Talia and the worry of getting caught, I think what a lucky idiot I am. Once, she spots me and frowns.

—m—

On the road between Cannes and Nice, Tommaso signals to me to pull in at a service station. 'We must buy food to eat on the way. It is too dangerous to stop for long.'

I glance at the fuel level. 'I'm going to fill up here. We need to stay topped up if we're going to try and make a run for it with Talia.'

Tommaso nods curtly. 'It will be best if you and Becks do the shopping. I don't wan' to scare the horses.'

As I fill up The Beast and Becks raids the

shelves in the service station shop, I find myself wondering at what Tommaso's just said. His words sound incredibly British and much older than he is – almost like something Dad would have jokingly said. I glance inside the car. Tommaso's head is rolled back against the head rest, like he's holding on so hard to this mission he has. What must he be thinking, so desperate to rescue this sister he's never met? And why is he on his own? Where's his father?

We drive on in a tense silence for several hundred kilometres. Signs to Rome start to appear with increasing frequency and despite the aircon, sweat starts to trickle down my back at the thought of some cop peering inside at us. Stuck at some roadworks, I have one of my ideas. So I rummage in all the glove boxes, cocktail cabinets and other gadgets that Bentleys just seem to love.

'What have you lost, Joe?' Becks' voice is on the sarcastic edge of concerned.

'Just trying to find some camo – ah, here we are!' Triumphantly, I retrieve a chauffeur's cap from the capacious glovebox, jam the cap on my head and fish out some shades that I've spotted in the door pocket.

'Would you like me to find you a false moustache?'

'C'mon Becks – you gotta admit I look a bit less like some idiot tearaway illegal driver now?'

'How about some idiot tearaway illegal driver pretending rather badly to be a chauffeur?'

We hear a kind of gasping noise coming from the seat beside me and I turn, alarmed that Tommaso is ill. But he's just shaking with laughter. He draws a deep breath. 'I am sorry – it is such a long time... Are you always this crazy double act?'

I concentrate on the road. 'Hadn't quite thought of it like that... have we, Becks?'

All I get is a snort of laughter from the back seat. But I keep going with the shades and the chauffeur cap. From a distance, they must give exactly the right impression.

—∞—

Eight hours later, the sun has set, I've taken off the shades, we've eaten the food, demolished most of the lemonade and made two more pit stops. We've also put in eight hundred kilometres since Marseille, and the signs are talking Genova, Firenze and Roma. But we haven't passed any border control. Although the route over the last hour has been interesting; hurtling down narrow tracks where I prayed we wouldn't meet a fifty tonner; and negotiating coast roads where there was nothing but a sheer drop to the sea far below. 'Tommaso, we've been following signs for Italian cities, yeah?'

'Correct, Joe. Would you like another break?' His voice is ironic.

'Nah, we want to get to Talia as fast as you do. But – does that mean we're actually in Italy now?'

'About two hundred kilometres from Rome.'

'But – what about the border controls?'

In the lights from passing headlamps, his face looks older than seventeen. 'I had hoped to find a way without the border police… we were lucky.'

'I know I look a joke of a chauffeur but we have our passports…?'

Tommaso's voice sounds way older than seventeen. 'Is not just the border police who are at the borders.'

Becks sits up in the back seat. 'You mean… the Mafia?'

'The Camorra.' Tommaso's lean face stares at the road. 'They are more powerful than the Mafia. There are many criminal clans in Italy, including the Andrangheta in Calabria in the South. But the Camorra is the deadliest and the biggest.'

'Have they always been more powerful than the Mafia?'

'Always. And operating mainly out of Napoli where there is a murder a day, at least.' Tommaso smiles slightly. 'Not like your English apple a day, is it? Not good for health?'

'So… we went round the border controls because the Camorra would have been there?'

Tommaso nods and his eyes close as he leans his head back; his right hand is never far away from the knife in his hip pocket. Fewer headlamps are coming in the opposite direction now. In the back seat, Becks' eyes flash in the passing beams. She's waiting for me to ask.

'Your dad, Tommaso. He, like, took you away

with him, didn't he? When you were very small? Because, your mum… the Contessa…'

'Poisoned people?' Tommaso rubs his eyes. 'Two years ago, my father told me I was a day old baby when he stole me from the private hospital, because my mother was a murderer who ran a drugs gang. Before that, he had always told me that she died of a long illness.'

'When did you find out about Talia?'

'At the same time, he told me I had a twin sister. But he could not even tell me her name.'

'So… ?'

Tommaso's lean, hungry face looks in the rear view mirror as we drive towards Rome. 'I was very angry with my father. I asked him why he did not take my sister as well.'

'What did he say?'

'He said my mother's guards were everywhere because she did not trust him anymore. What kind of excuse is that?'

Becks says quietly, 'Tommaso, sometimes hard choices have to be made.'

Tommaso's voice is like iron. 'I made that hard choice for myself. I ran away from my father and went to Napoli.'

'And that was for good, was it? You never went back?

'I never went back.'

I brake hard at the flashing blue lights of a traffic accident and steer round it. I think we're on a high coast road but I can no way see beyond the edge; just guess at the limitless drop beneath. The Bentley's headlamps cut a tunnel of brightness through the night. 'What happened in Napoli?'

Tommaso's voice is tired. 'I found a new family.'

I glance across at him. His eyes are closing. I whisper, 'Was your new family the Camorra?'

He nods. And still that frail hand embraces the knife. 'I had to find out about Talia. The Camorra know everything that is going on. I went to work for them.'

'What sort of stuff did you do?'

'First, they taught me to drive their garbage trucks. They have many businesses, especially garbage full of toxic waste. And I was also… come si dice?' He slides his hand out from my jacket and he's holding my wallet. 'Borsaiolo…'

Becks' voice is admiring. 'A rather good pickpocket…?'

He deftly replaces the wallet. 'My thanks, Becks Bowman. I will remember your recommendation for my next job interview.'

Becks leans forward. 'How did you find out about Talia?'

'I made myself so useful, none of them could do without me. They were always wanting me to take a message here, lift that guy's wallet, drive this armoured car to wherever. So I was not popular with kids my age.'

I take in the bruises on his skinny arms. 'Fights?'

He shrugs. 'Every day.'

'But you got your information?'

Tommaso smiles that thin smile. 'Kidnapping is the number one hot subject with the Camorra when they're not talking about who is to be taken out next. I became very good at being invisible.'

'What did you find out?'

The familiar blue eyes take me in. 'That my not so beloved father was operating in the same shadows as me.'

I'm feeling cold. 'What d'you mean, Tommaso?'

'Snooping around an office one day, I found an email from my father to the Napoli Camorra boss. It contained a date, a time, a location and the name *Zeitgeist*. It seemed pretty clear that this was some kind of codename and the person was a target.'

Tommaso's eyes gaze forward into the night. I have to look at the road. But in the rear view mirror, Becks' eyes meet mine. And we're hearing Monsieur's words as he stares into the stone fireplace at L'Étoile: *Zeitgeist has disappeared with no trace.*

—⁓—

As pale strands of pink cloud are just starting to show above the wooded hills around Rome, Tommaso sits up and consults the sat nav on his mobile. 'Good. There will be less traffic around at this time.'

'What's the speed limit in Rome?'

Tommaso grabs a nectarine from the carrier bag and bites into it. 'You don' need to know, Joe Grayling.'

I hesitate before asking him such a private sort of question. 'Tommaso, you don't have to tell me, 'course you don't, but what nationality is your dad?'

He wipes nectarine juice from his mouth and looks back to his sat nav. 'What makes you ask?'

'Well… it's not just that your English is so good but you said something so English… 'I don't want to scare the horses'? That's the kind of thing my dad would have said.'

'Then let us just say that my father was as English as yours, Joe Grayling.' He looks steadily at the display on his phone and I turn my attention to the streets of Rome. Even at 4.30 in the morning, they're manic. But in the blast of horns and mazes of traffic lights, part of my mind lingers on Tommaso's 'was as English as yours, Joe Grayling'. Has he pushed his father so far out of his life that 'was' is all there is? Or is his father dead, like mine?

—⁂—

As soon as we're through Rome, Tommaso's instructions become terser. He steers us up ever more minor roads until we're in a forest of tall pine trees. The track has become nothing but gigantic potholes and the Bentley is wallowing through them like a tanker in a rough sea. Tommaso punches a button on his sat nav phone. 'We are the nearest we can get to her by car.'

As we get out, flexing stiff muscles, bird song echoes through the pine trees. I wonder where

Corbo is now. The sky through the trees is slowly turning a more pinky grey, but nestling on the horizon are some puffy, ink-black clouds.

'Is upwards, now.'

Becks stares at the wooded terrain. 'Where are we?'

'On a mountain above Rome. Now, please follow quietly!'

We follow him through miles of pinewoods that go steadily uphill. The ground becomes harder, and in between the trees we climb over rocks. And all the time there's this birdsong, echoing through the trees. Higher notes and lower, squawkier ones, like Corbo.

I whisper to Tommaso, 'How did you know where she is?'

He stares ahead through the trees. 'They bring many kidnap victims up here. Often, I am the one who guards them.'

I feel very cold at the thought of Tommaso standing over captives with a gun. What else have the Camorra forced him to do?

As the sun creeps above the fat dark clouds, flies start to buzz around our heads and we swat them away. Becks exclaims, 'God these midges are worse than the ones in Aix!' Quite suddenly, all the bird song goes quiet. There's a pause of maybe two seconds, then a vortex of wing beats as huge flocks of birds lift off from the trees, wheel and call in the air, then head in the opposite direction from those dark clouds.

Shivering in his thin shirt, Tommaso leads us onwards through rustling, knee-high ferns. Once, I think I catch a faint rumble of thunder. Is it those growing cloud banks? Becks touches my arm. 'What was that?'

'Vesuvius?'

'Very funny!'

Tommaso turns, his young-old face looking drawn in the weak dawn light. 'Probably just thunder. But the birds have gone because they can sense the beginnings of a small local earthquake.'

'Are you serious?'

'Of course.' He struggles on up the slope, breathing hard. Sometimes a shower of insects erupts from the ferns and buzzes over our heads. Once, I grab a branch to pull myself up the slope and look at my hand just in time to shake off an inch-long black scorpion that's hitched a ride. At that moment, the skies go black and we can hardly see in front of us. We switch on our phone torches; the thin beams cut through the dark as we stumble on.

Suddenly, there's a rumble like an express train right beneath our feet. The whole forest is full of the roaring as we're thrown to the ground. Somewhere very close, there's a creaking. Tommaso gives me and Becks a huge shove. 'Get out the way!' We roll clear as a pine tree topples, crashing against its neighbours.

In the dim light, Becks' face is pale. 'That was a bit close…'

Tommaso is quiet as he checks his sat nav, and I have a feeling that he knows more about small local earthquakes than he's letting on. 'The place is not far now.'

'Do you know what it looks like?'

'An old woodcutter's hut. And they will be everywhere.'

We press on up the slope, listening out for any more falling trees. It's eerily quiet without the birdsong. Just the whispering of ferns and dead leaves beneath our feet. The weird daytime darkness is lifting slightly when Tommaso stops and whispers, 'Can you see it, up ahead?'

The wooden hut is just visible through the trees. The one small window has no glass in it and the hut is dark inside. 'God, Tommaso – let's get her out of there!'

We flit our way from one tree to the next. In front of the hut is a small clearing where there's no cover at all; just the shadows of trees in the slow grey dawn. Tommaso whispers, 'Wait here... I will go first.'

That's when the torches blaze in our eyes and we look at guns that are looking at us. There are three of them. One is a woman, middle-aged, in a black blouse and skirt. Her grey hair is strained back into a ragged ponytail. She steps forward and holds a small pistol to Tommaso's head. Her voice is hoarse, like she smokes a pack a day. 'Baby come home, eh?'

Tommaso never moves. 'An' jus' look what I bring you, Donna Maria.'

She laughs; a hard cackle, harsher than any crow. There's a click as she releases the safety catch. Paralysed with horror, all Becks and I can do is watch. Then one of the men moves quickly and smashes his gun down on her wrist. With a wallop, the bullet ploughs into the ground, sending up a spout of dust. She starts to scream at him in Italian and he's shouting back. I dart a quick look at Tommaso to see if it could be a good time to make a move. He gives a slight shake of the head.

We all jump as a burst of gunfire brings a tree branch crashing to the ground, and the taller of the two men comes forward from the shadows. He holds a smoking Magnum. In the dim light, I see a hawk-like nose and eyes as pale and bright as silver coins with nothing behind them. He wears a black Stetson and a long black Mac. Claw-like spurs glitter at his jack-booted heels. Instantly, the squabbling man and woman shut up. Boss man waves the Magnum towards the hut. That's when I catch a glimpse of the machine gun slung round his back and the belts full of ammo. More guns dig into our backs as we're pushed inside. In the dark, I look around for Talia but she's not there. So this was a trap all along.

—m—

They tie me and Becks to the rafters, our arms stretched above our heads. The smaller man and the woman drag Tommaso out through the door.

He cranes his head back to flash me a look that I'll never forget. Then the butt of the woman's gun hits his back, making him stagger.

Stetson pauses, thoughtfully spinning the chambers of the Magnum. There's a slight smile on his face as he looks at us. His voice is dry and very English, like he's ordering afternoon tea in a stately home. 'Now, my dear young people, there is one way – and one way only – in which you can leave this place, apart from in body bags. You can tell me who you are.' He strolls over to Becks and strokes her hair. 'So pretty…' Becks' foot lands a kick boxing number on his knee; I hear the crack and see him wince. 'Feisty, are we? Not always a quality to be commended.'

'Get stuffed, perv!'

'Unwise to be so unhelpful, my dear. Unless your gallant boyfriend feels like being rather more forthcoming than you are.'

'Get stuffed perv hits the spot for me, thanks.'

'You know, sonny, that really was not a good choice of words.' He slams his Magnum into my shoulder but I've already braced myself. I can hear Dad's voice telling me to shut my big mouth because this man has reinvented dangerous and he has a short fuse. And it comes as a shock that I can hear Dad's voice once again.

Mr Irritable shrugs. 'I shan't waste bullets on you, my dears. The aftershocks will sort things nicely, with no need for tedious forensic calling cards. Ciao.' To help things along, he whips the machine gun from his back and in a thunderous burst of fire takes out half the door frame, before strolling through what's left of it without a backwards glance.

CHAPTER 6

A Darker Place

In the bitter smoke and dust, we cough and wheeze. 'Tommaso sold us out!'

'No, Becks! He saved our lives. If he hadn't made like he was going to hand us over, we'd all have been shot like rats. My guess is he's in far more danger than we are – Talia, too.'

There's a sudden roar like a huge truck rushing past outside and the ground shakes again. The wrecked door frame creaks and sags. Groaning, the ceiling takes on more of a slope.

'If this rafter would just break!'

'It won't break until the ceiling comes down – on us.'

'If I could just get at my phone…'

'It's not the answer to everything, Becks.'

'Alright, Mister Clever, YOU think of something!'

Another truck. The door frame buckles and collapses in a heap of firewood. With a huge CRACK! the wooden wall splits and the roof is now only two feet above our heads. Dust showers into our eyes from the rotten rafter.

'Shit, Joe – I've had this!'

'Becks, shush! Listen!'

With our eyes streaming, we can hardly see a thing. But there's an eerie silence after the last shock, broken by a single, long 'Aagh!' I stare towards the small window. Dark wings flap impatiently.

'It's Corbo! Maybe he can go for help.'

'Correction, Joe. He IS the help!'

As Becks speaks, Corbo flutters down onto the rafter and starts to attack the ropes with his savage beak. I bet crows could have won wars for us if we'd known how to recruit them. In less than five minutes, we're free. The dark bird flies to the window and looks back at us, his head on one side, eyes bright; then, he flies. We throw ourselves after him, scrambling through splintered wood and choking dust. As Becks squeezes herself through the window, the mother of all express trains beneath us sends the hut ceiling on its final journey.

Becks' legs disappear. I launch myself, wriggle frantically and tumble out beside her onto the dry leaves. There's a mighty crash as the rafter lands where I was a couple of seconds ago, with the full weight of the roof above it.

'Now what?' Becks brushes dust off her jeans.

'Dunno. Where the hell would they have gone? And is Talia where they're taking Tommaso?'

'Joe – look at Corbo!' The raven is sitting on a branch at eye level with us. Then, he lifts off, always in the same direction, wheels and comes back to the branch. Impatiently, he chatters at us. The feathers on his neck stand up like a lion's mane. 'He wants us to follow him, Joe.'

Corbo cries his 'Aagh!' again and fixes us with bright eyes.

Becks yanks her dusty mane of red hair into a pony tail. 'Let's go!'

'But we save this location along with the location of the Bentley before we move a foot, OK?'

'Deal.'

—ɯ—

Like a dark spirit, Corbo flits from branch to branch, turning and looking at me and Becks as we stumble after him through the trees and up the mountain. The sky gets slowly lighter. But always there are the trucks and sometimes the express trains of Tommaso's small local earthquakes. It feels like the ground is constantly re-arranging itself under our feet. We stay upright, but only just.

'When is it ever going to stop?'

Corbo shrieks at us from a branch, flapping angry wings. 'We have to keep going, Becks – we don't know how much time we have.'

'But what do we do if we catch up with them? They've got guns.'

'Haven't a clue – but we have to know where they are and Corbo seems to, doesn't he?'

We must have been struggling up the mountain for another twenty minutes when we hit a steep downwards slope which is nothing but loose stones.

Instantly, my feet start to slide. I grab at a branch but it snaps off in my hand. Becks is sliding behind me. 'Can't stop!'

I start a spread-eagled toboggan down the slope, sharp stones cutting into my back, my eyes full of dust. Suddenly, there's nothing left of the slope. For maybe half a second I'm flying. I open my arms to grab at anything, find a thousand needles and cling on because my life depends on it. Becks is doing the same just below me. I used to climb bus shelters, but I've never been at the top of a pine tree before. 'You OK Becks?'

'Going down! Shit, my hands!'

'Try and wrap your legs round!'

'YOU try it!'

Fighting with feet, hands, arms and legs to slow our bumpy slide down the pine tree, we crash to the rocky ground at the bottom and survey the battle damage. Hands are not in good shape and my top has a Z-shaped rip at the front, but I never liked it anyway.

From high up in the tree, Corbo calls. We look around at the pit we've toppled into, with its rocky walls in their pink stone. A few skinny pine trees like the one that saved us grow straight up from the pit floor. The cliff walls tower above us. Beyond them, the grey clouds let through a few random beams of pale sunshine. And it's weirdly quiet again. No express trains but still no birdsong either. Becks looks up into the tree and in a quiet voice calls Corbo.

The dark bird flutters down to where we're sat, getting our breath back. Then he takes purposeful crow strides towards the rock face. And for the first time, I notice the small hole that could be a cave entrance at the base of the cliff.

'Joe...' Becks isn't looking at the rocks. I follow her gaze to a pine tree about thirty feet away and see a part of Tommaso's shoulder and arm beyond the trunk, like he's leaning on it. But he's completely still. I look at Becks and all the colour has gone from her face. I feel as cold as winter. Taking Becks' hand, I go with her to Tommaso's tree. As we walk round it, we can see that his eyes are wide open and staring at the hole that might be a cave. Our hearts have nearly stopped when he whispers, 'She is in there.'

'Is she alright?' Becks and I speak at exactly the same time.

'I don't know.'

Becks glances at the cave entrance. 'Are they...?'

'They have gone.'

I look closely at Tommaso. 'Are you sure? Why have they gone?'

Like he's coming out of a trance, he looks at us for the first time. 'I am sure. I will tell you later. And now we must go to Talia together. Otherwise, she will think I am just another of them....'

Becks whispers, 'She must be terrified...'

And all I can think is, 'If she's still alive.'

The three of us and one noisy raven flying from branch to branch slowly approach the cave. Then, when all we can still see is the blackness of the cave mouth, Tommaso calls in a low voice. 'Talia, mia cara sorella. Sono Tommaso, tuo fratello. Sono qui con i tuoi amici, Joe e Becks. Venga e sia sicura!'

I don't need to understand Italian to get the gist of what Tommaso is saying. Seconds pass and there's no sound from within the cave. Sunbeams move through the trees, slowly coming and going. Corbo flaps impatient wings. Becks whispers, 'Let us go first, Tommaso.' She steps quietly into the cave and we follow, flicking on our phone torches. The floor of the cave is strewn with pine needles and we keep stumbling over boulders. A sudden dull rumble beneath our feet makes us freeze, terrified that we'll all be trapped in this hole forever. But it passes, and we move on into the darkness.

'What's that?' My torch beam has picked out something that looks like a rag, lying across a boulder.

Becks touches it. 'It's a dress. A very small one…'

Then Tommaso's torch lights on something that makes me wish I was asleep and dreaming. It's a tiny child's skull with a hole where the mouth and half the jaw used to be. One eye is closed and the other is open, dangling out of its socket. I'm starting to shake when Becks picks it up. 'It's a doll… or it was, once.'

Tommaso turns to us, barely glancing at the skull. 'I know what you are thinking. You are right.'

'They take children?'

'All the more reason to find Talia…' His shadow melts into the darkness, his footsteps almost silent.

Becks moves swiftly past me to catch up with him. 'Tommaso, we need to call out for her – she must be hiding, absolutely petrified.'

'Then it must be you and Joe this time.'

Becks stands motionless. 'Talia – it's Becks and Joe, your mates! We have Tommaso your brother with us! He's come to get you out of here!'

In the silence, all we can hear is the echo... 'here, here, here.'

'Talia – please! Let your brother help you!'

'... you, you, you.'

And then we hear it. A low, quiet sobbing. As though a heart is breaking. The cave air moves around us as Tommaso rushes towards the sound. High above us there's a myriad beat of tiny wings as hundreds of bats take flight. Becks and I follow, fearful of what we might find. Her torch picks out a hollow in the cave wall where tattered blankets and sleeping bags lie on the floor. An empty plastic water bottle crunches under my shoe. And there is Tommaso, gently helping Talia to her feet. She's still in the pyjamas she must have been wearing when she was dragged from the hospital, and her face is so pale. But Tommaso is whispering to her in Italian and brushing the tears away from her eyes like a mother might have done, if they'd both ever had a mother who loved them. She turns to us as we approach. Then her eyes close and Tommaso catches her as she falls. With an extraordinary strength, he lifts his sister into his arms. 'Andiamo!'

My phone torch packs up as soon as we set

71

off back towards the cave entrance, but thankfully Becks' is still working and I grab Tommaso's from him as he carries Talia through the shadows. Just as a faint light from the cave mouth starts to glimmer on the rock walls, Talia moans quietly and Tommaso lowers her carefully to the ground. 'I think she's coming round.'

Becks takes her hand. 'It's OK Talia – we're getting you out of here.'

But Talia is looking only at Tommaso. 'My mother told me once that I had a brother… a twin brother. I thought it was just to be cruel.'

'It was cruel.' Tommaso takes her other hand. 'But it was true. Now we must go!'

She turns to us. 'Arnaud… is he alright?'

Becks squeezes her hand. 'You'll soon be back with him, Talia!' Tommaso puts a supporting arm around his sister as we begin the descent down the mountain.

—m—

All the way back through the forest, I see guns behind every tree. The birds still haven't returned after the quake, so the only sound is our feet on the pine needles and our whispered conversations. Becks and I walk together to give the twins some much needed time with each other. 'D'you think Tommaso knows that their mother is dead?'

Becks takes my hand. 'I would guess so – what doesn't he know? Did he tell you why Top Gun and crew had gone?'

'No. And now ain't the time to ask, is it?'

She shakes her head. 'Course not. Have we got the Bentley co-ords?'

'Hell – my battery's packed up.'

Becks contemplates her mobile. 'Just as well that I made a note?'

'Is your real name Moneypenny?'

'I think it's time we called Monsieur, don't you?'

'Oh God – he's going to be furious.'

'He'd be more furious if we were dead, wouldn't he?'

'Er…'

She punches the keys. 'OK, I'll make the call.'

'You will not get a signal in these mountains.' Tommaso hurries up to us, holding Talia's hand. 'And you could be overheard trying.'

Becks switches her phone off. 'Are they still after us then? What's going on, Tommaso?'

He runs a hand through lanky blond hair. 'There is no time to explain now, I am sorry Becks. They have the one person they wanted above all, but that won't stop them from coming back for us.'

—⁂—

The birds have returned to the trees by the time we reach the Bentley, but the song is very muted. I'm amazed that the car's still there and hasn't been swallowed up in some giant earthquake. Becks and Talia get in the back and I'm about to climb into the driver's seat, when I see Tommaso reaching beneath the offside rear wheelarch. 'Is there a problem, Tommaso? Some damage?'

'Maybe some company that we don't want.'

'Our friends could have left a tracker?' I go to the nearside rear wheelarch but my searching hands find nothing. Tommaso wriggles the upper half of his body right underneath the Bentley. I look around uneasily, dying to get out of here, straining to hear any feet on leaves; but the forest is silent apart from the subdued chirps from the trees.

'Eccolo!' Emerging from beneath the car, Tommaso holds up a small plastic case with two huge magnets on the underside and an on/off switch.

'So, we switch it off?'

'Not yet. That would tell them immediately that we're onto their game. They could get more of their people after us then.' Tommaso speaks in a low voice and it's easy to guess that he doesn't want to frighten Talia. 'I think we turn it off in Rome.'

'That makes sense – plenty of possible reasons why, yeah?'

Tommaso smiles his thin smile. 'You are beginning to think like a Camorristo, Joe.'

'Will they know if we take this thing into the car with us?'

'The device is not that sophisticated.'

The Bentley's mighty engine purrs into life and we slip away from that shuddering mountain with its dark forests and secret caves. And Tommaso's words gnaw steadily at my mind with every mile we drive. *They have the one person they wanted above all…*

The tracker lies between Tommaso's feet as we take the road to Rome. A green light next to the on/off switch flashes relentlessly. I wonder who's looking at the signal. And what they're thinking of doing about it.

In the back seat, Becks and Talia talk in murmurs. Becks is getting Talia to drink some water and telling her that she'll soon see Arnaud. Safe enough ground. Whereas the questions I need to ask Tommaso could produce more earthquakes. So I try a more cautious tack. 'Tommaso – about Corbo? He like, saved our lives when we were stuck in that hut. How did he know where to find us?'

Tommaso looks steadily at the road ahead. 'I found Corbo when I was driving my first garbage lorry for my new Camorra family. I had stopped to empty some bins when I saw some kids kicking a small dark bird around in the dust.'

'How many of them were there?'

He closes tired eyes. 'May two or three?'

'So you like, sorted them out?'

'They were not expecting anyone to be so angry about them beating up a baby crow. They laughed and they went away.'

'And your Camorra family – what did they think?' I'm remembering the time when I announced to Mum that I wanted a pet rat.

'They shoot everything they don't like so they have never known about Corbo. I keep scrap food in my pockets for him. He's with me a lot, when it's safe.'

'So did you like, send him to find us in that hut?'

He shakes his head. 'The crow family has the greatest brains of any birds. The raven especially. And Corbo had met you and Becks so he could track you. I am not surprised that he got you both out of there.'

'And brought us to you?'

'He always knows where I am.' That thin smile again. 'Maybe he thinks I am a poor old raven who can't fly or make a racket like he does!'

'That's pretty amazing… to have a raven for a mate…'

'He's a bit of a nag sometimes.' Another so English, so Dad way of speaking.

'We noticed. So, where is he now?'

'He doesn't like travelling. He only came to the chateau because he knew I would need him. Now, I think he is going back into the forests where he belongs.'

'Will you see Corbo again?' Becks has been listening to everything.

Tommaso turns his thin face to her. 'That is his choice. We were friends to each other at a time of great loneliness for us both.' He looks at the sleeping Talia and whispers. 'How is she?'

'I'm a bit worried about this medication Arnaud said she has to take every day. We need to call the hospital as soon as we get back.'

'But she is not going back there!'

'No way – we can look after her at the chateau. She'll be safe there.'

'There is so much you have to tell me about Talia, isn't there?'

In the mirror, I see Becks hold his gaze. Her voice is gentle, 'And there's a lot that you have to tell us about you, isn't there, Tommaso?'

He says nothing but steadily meets Becks' look. I feel a sharp pity for Talia's thin, bruised brother. And a fear of what he might have to tell.

—w—

'We are approaching Rome in daylight, Joe, so it will be different. You must drive exactly as I say!'

After about five minutes of driving exactly like Tommaso says, I work out that the rule in Rome is Bat out of Hell. Pedestrians step out in front of the traffic where there are no crossings and just look the driver in the eye. Sometimes the driver stops. And sometimes they accelerate, right at the pedestrians. And when pedestrians cross in great crowds on a real crossing, all the cars just charge at them like foxes on a turkey farm. And the sound effects are much the same. So now I know why Tommaso told me that there was no point in knowing what the speed limit is in Rome. At one random set of traffic lights, he whispers to me, 'I'm going to switch off the tracker now.'

'OK, do it'. It's like being let out of a prison where everyone's watching you.

An hour later, Rome is far behind, it's getting dark and I spot the cheerful lights of a service station. 'Tommaso, surely it's safe now? The tracker's switched off.'

His voice is deadly tired. 'I am very sorry, Joe, but it is not safe here.'

Biting hunger makes me speak out of turn. 'Who is this person they've got? Is that why they let you and Talia go?'

'Joe.' Becks' voice holds a warning note. 'I think all this is going to have to wait. Right now, let's just get back in one piece, yeah?'

Shamed into gut aching silence, I turn my attention to the rear view mirror. No one behind. Another hour into the drive and I think we must be nearing the border between Italy and France. Following Tommaso's directions, I've been driving the same coast road that we came by. But up ahead, some blue lights are flashing and I don't remember them.

'Is this a border control?'

Tommaso's voice is hard as iron. 'Don't slow down – go faster!'

'But there's a barrier… and men…'

'With guns. Drive, Joe Grayling! Becks and Talia, get your heads down, now!'

I can hear Becks looking after Talia as I floor the accelerator. In a few seconds we're doing 80 and I steer the Bentley at the barrier. A dude jumps right into the middle of the road, pointing a gun at my head. Praying that this machine has bullet proof glass like Precious did, I drive straight at him like they do in Rome. As he dives for cover, his bullet takes out the right hand door mirror and glass explodes like fireworks. The Bentley smashes head on into the barrier and it disintegrates into the night.

'Faster! They will not let it go at that!'

I hurl the Bentley along the coast road. Many hundreds of feet below lies the Mediterranean. I glance in the rear view mirror. No lights behind us, yet.

Becks whispers, 'I'm going to call Monsieur, Joe!'

'Yeah, do that.' I hit a bend that keeps on tightening up.

'Can't get a signal!'

'Keep trying.'

—∞—

Two hours later, we're back on French coast roads. A full moon beams down onto the sea below. Becks has been talking to Monsieur for the last few minutes, filling him in on everything that's happened since he and Arnaud went to see Le Loup. 'We've just passed Nice and we're about ten kilometres from Cannes.'

Thinking back to my first goes in a Bentley, I flip up the centre console lid. All the hands-free connections are there. 'Plug it in, Becks. Then we can all hear.'

What we can all hear is Monsieur's voice with

a fury so quiet, it's worse than if he was shouting at the top of his voice. 'On no account must you continue to Cannes!'

'But we got away from them, Monsieur. We switched off the tracker.'

'Not before you had given them everything they needed.'

'What d'you mean, Monsieur?'

'They know exactly your direction and the car you are in. Do you really want those rocket launchers behind you again?'

His words shock me back into reality as I see those deadly fireworks arcing over our car and exploding just in front of us. 'No! So… what do we do?'

'You do what they are *not* expecting! You come off the Corniche at the next junction. As soon as you have left the main coast road, you find a place to stop and call me. By then, I will have more instructions for you. Tu comprends?'

'Oui Monsieur.'

'Vas-y Joe!'

'This Monsieur knows things, doesn't he?' Tommaso' voice holds a note of cautious respect.

'He's saved our lives more than once, Tommaso.'

Becks says, 'There are headlights behind us, closing fast.'

The lights are blazing in my mirror. A flicker of red behind us is all it takes to convince me that we have shooters after us. 'Heads down and hang on!' I kick the Bentley up to 120 mph, braking hard before every hairpin bend then powering away into the next straight. Gradually, the headlights fall back and I marvel at the grip of the black beast as I fling the steering wheel from side to side. The exit looms. Without indicating, I blast up it, decelerating to 20 mph in around 3 seconds, seatbelts biting into our ribs. The pursuing car hasn't got the brakes to follow us. I pull off the road beneath some trees and switch off the headlights. Tommaso whispers, 'They will leave at the next exit and come for us the other way.'

'So it's not bad that we stay where we are?'

'If we can get further away from the road, it will help.'

I tuck the Bentley in a bit more and call Monsieur.

'Can you give me your sat nav co-ordinates?'

Becks checks her phone and reels them off.

'Good. Now I am going to give you a set of co-ordinates which will take you to a location just outside the boundary of La Croisette heliport. You need to find the perimeter fence and then call me. And, Joe?'

'Monsieur?'

'Were you pursued to your current location?'

'They took a shot at us but we got ahead and they couldn't make the exit.'

'I am afraid that this route will take you eight kilometres along the only road they can use to get to you, coming in the opposite direction. It will be extremely dangerous before you take the turn to the heliport. Now go!'

The moon sails out from behind the clouds as we take the coast road. The terrain is hilly and full of bends that suddenly turn into twisting cobras. Most of the time we're horribly near a precipitous drop to the sea below. Out of the dark, a headlamp glow appears ahead of us on the horizon. Tommaso whispers, 'If we can see their headlamps, they can see ours. Switch them off Joe! The moon is enough to see by.'

'Good plan.' I turn off the bright Xenons and readjust my eyes to moonlight.

'It is a well used Camorra tactic.'

The oncoming beams get brighter, then very bright. Sweeping round a bend, what looks like a black Merc dazzles us before flashing by. Its brake lights blaze on and I slam the accelerator to the floor. 'Is that one of theirs, d'you think?'

'Could be. Could also be police who don't like a car driving without lights.'

'But he'll have to find a place to turn…'

'We have that on our side, yes. If we can just get to the heliport turn before they catch up…'

'How far did Monsieur say?'

'He said eight kilometres… must be about three now.'

Signs loom up, flash past and disappear into the dark as I drive at terrifying speeds through z-bends, up steep hill climbs and down precipitous descents. Then my blood goes cold as I see a dim glow behind us. At that moment, Talia calls, 'There is the turn off to the heliport – I know it well…' She stops and

I guess it's bringing back memories of her wealthy but unloved life with the Contessa. And I have a feeling that Tommaso knows this territory well too, but for different reasons.

The glow's getting brighter. 'I'm going to lose speed now and take the turn without braking because that would be a dead giveaway. So hang on!'

We're doing 120, then 90, then 60 as the turn appears. It's a sharp left hander but thankfully nothing's coming our way as I swing through on the accelerator, tyres talking merrily, and power on down the narrow road.

'Can we switch on the headlamps yet?' Becks' voice is concerned. 'Only we're nearly there, and we have to look for this perimeter fence?'

Tommaso exclaims, 'I can see it – look, over there. The moon is shining on the barbed wire.'

'Joe, we're there. Can you find a place to stop?'

I pull onto the dusty verge, switch off the engine and make a call. 'We're at the location, Monsieur.'

'There is a gap where someone cut through the perimeter fence a while ago.'

We get out and run along the fence. The ground is rough, and we use the slim beams of our phone torches. In the distance I can hear an engine but it's over our heads.

Tommaso waves us towards him. The gap is a small one. He's prising the wire mesh apart and kicking it down.

'We're at the hole in the fence, Monsieur.'

'Go straight through and wait no more than ten metres beyond.'

The engine noise gets louder and turns into spluttering machine gun fire as the black copter drops from the sky, churning up clouds of dust. The rotors slow as a figure jumps to the ground and races towards us. 'Quickly, all of you!'

Behind Monsieur, Arnaud climbs out and waves urgently at us. Tommaso and Becks lift Talia between them and dash towards the copter.

'You too, Joe – give me the car key!'

Funny, but my feet won't move. 'If your plan is to draw their fire then I'm coming with you Monsieur.'

'Absolutely not!'

'Sorry, Monsieur. I got you into this and I'm coming with you.'

'Joe, this is not the time for pig-headedness!'

'Au contraire, Monsieur – you know that two of us will be better than one if we want to give these bad men a run for their money. Yeah?'

Talia, Tommaso and Becks are in the copter. Arnaud is revving the rotors but they're all still waiting for the fourth passenger. The moonlight glints on the short cropped silver hair of this man who has been like a father to me, all the time I've been looking for mine. Monsieur looks straight at me for a nano-second. Then he turns to the copter and waves both arms above his head. The rotors roar. It lifts off into the night.

CHAPTER 7

Point Blank

We run to the Bentley. 'You are a hard man to argue with Joe. And you are right, I need a crew who knows what he's doing.'

'So no headlights? And we get back to the main road before we switch the tracker on?'

He nods, waving me into the driving seat. 'Do you think they saw you on your way here?'

I tell him about the Merc and the following glow. At the junction, Monsieur tells me to take a left towards Nice. The road is quiet, nothing ahead or behind. After a few miles he switches the tracker back on. 'The clock is ticking now.'

'What do we want them to think, Monsieur?'

His voice is grim. 'That they still have a chance of sending you and Becks and the twins to oblivion.'

'Why? Is it just that the Camorra don't like anyone who isn't them?'

'This is not just about the Camorra, Joe. A power even more lethal is leading this, from what Becks has told me about your encounter with the gun man.'

'Is it to do with the network?'

He stares at the dark road ahead, the moon occasionally shimmering on the tarmac. 'It is always to do with the network, when traditional methods of righting wrongs fail. The problem is…' Monsieur's usually authoritative voice tails away.

'It's IN the network now, isn't it Monsieur?'

'I'm afraid it has been there for a long time, Joe.'

'How far does it go back?'

His voice is cautious. 'I think, seventeen years.'

'When I was born, and Becks, and Arnaud and Talia and Tommaso. Everything always comes back to that time, doesn't it, Monsieur?'

He's quiet for a few seconds before he says, 'Talia's brother is bearing a terrible burden. As soon as we get back to L'Étoile, we must share that weight with him.'

'How d'you know this, Monsieur?'

'Something Le Loup said, when Arnaud and I went to see him in Avignon.'

'Oh, and Tommaso told us his father….'

'Joe.' Monsieur's voice is urgent and instantly I see what he's looking at. We're driving the coast road, cliffs on our right, the Mediterranean on our left, a thousand feet below. A bright beam rakes the cliffs. Above is a copter. And the beam is coming our way.

'Keep going. They will be looking for a moving target. With our headlamps off we will instantly attract their attention.'

'Did you think they'd have a copter?'

'Definitely. Which made it essential to undertake this petit divertissement.'

I swallow. 'Well, we've got speed on our side.'

'And something else entirely unknown to them, Joe.'

Monsieur switches on the radio. But we don't get FM. Out of the corner of my eye, I see the sat nav display change to a plan view of the Bentley. It looks like a computer game, with two weapon emplacements at the front of the car and four at the back. He opens a hatch in the footwell, takes out a joystick and presses a button. Instantly, the split-screen display shows a detailed view of the road ahead and behind.

'Heat seeking cameras, Monsieur?'

He nods. The copter is almost overhead now and the beam is firmly on the road. We've hit an unusually straight stretch. We'll be seen in a matter of seconds. Monsieur presses another button on the joystick and the display changes to just the road in front. A view finder has also appeared in the centre of the display. At the same time, a compartment just above the windscreen that looks like a sunglasses holder swings down to open up into a quietly beeping radar display.

The bright shaft of light from the copter sweeps over us, dazzling me momentarily. 'Use the screen to see, Joe!' Monsieur's hand moves towards what I thought was a cupholder slot, but no cupholder glides out. Inside the small, varnished wood tray is a single red button.

I glance in the rear view mirror and see the copter's beam switch off; the navigation lights disappear into the moonlit sky. 'D'you think it's armed?'

'Probably. But these are merely the gamekeepers sent to find the prey. They will be radioing our co-ordinates to the hunters.'

'So, they're just like Bertolini and the Contessa, aren't they? They get a kick out of this!'

Monsieur looks ahead at the road. The moonlight is gently shining on the tarmac and casting a silky sheen across the horizon of the Mediterranean. He says softly, 'Just remember that right now, we are controlling what they do. We have taken them off the trail they were on.'

'So they had that copter because they thought...'

'That there would be some kind of flight involved. But because you switched off the tracker in Rome, they could have wasted valuable time at Rome airport. And we seem to have got the timing right with the take off tonight.'

'So they think everyone's on board this car, right?'

'That is what we are aiming for, Joe.'

As he speaks, the radar bleeps more urgently. Something is closing very fast behind us. 'How far away is it?'

He switches on the split screen night vision and looks again at the radar. 'About two miles. But something is also approaching from in front.'

'Could just be any random car, couldn't it?'

'It is possible. But at this time of night on the Corniche...' He presses a button on the joystick and the display changes to Systems Check mode. Glancing at it, I see messages coming up like Ground to Air, Range Check, Range Absolute… then I have to look back at the road. But there can't be any doubt about it. 'This is a Bentley gunship isn't it, Monsieur?'

He smiles that half-smile. 'It certainly is not a rich man's toy, Joe. Now, concentrate. We are about to see some action.' He's watching the radar where the two dots are converging on us, one much faster than the other. Suddenly the dashboard screen switches to Bentley gunship mode and the two weapon emplacements at the front of the car are flashing. The viewfinder gives a continuously changing reading which I guess must be distance. Monsieur presses a button on the joystick. The radar bleep gets faster. Monsieur's hand reaches for the red button in its varnished wood tray. 'Do not brake or accelerate, Joe.' The radar signal turns into one long beep and Monsieur presses the red button. At the same time as a streak of red light soars from in front of the car, it's like we've hit a wall. 'The recoil. It will correct. Keep a steady speed.' A few seconds and we're driving normally again. A second more and there's a white light on the horizon, followed by a distant WHUMPH.

I'm not sure what to think. 'Have we like, blown them up, Monsieur?'

His voice is steady. 'We don't play this game the way they do, Joe. This was a deterrent which should do the job.'

'What about the dudes behind?'

'About now, they will be taking aim with their rocket launchers. And it's not going to happen.' Monsieur selects one of the rear weapon stations with the joystick. A tag comes up on the screen which just says **H**. He hits the red button and I can't see that anything's happening. Then he selects the station next to **H,** called **F**, and presses the button again. This time I see clouds of grey smoke gush in our rear, filling the sky behind us.

'Ah, I got it Monsieur! First oil, then smoke?'

'Not favourable for steering, let alone taking aim.'

The plume of smoke from up ahead is getting closer. Instinctively, I lose speed. 'Do we have to drive past this, Monsieur? There's no turning?'

'There is no turning.'

I glance at the radar. There's still more than one object in front of us. 'Is that the car?'

'The aim was to the front of the car, within ten metres. I cannot guarantee that there is no one there, Joe. The car is still within radar range.'

We have cliffs on the right and a sheer drop to the sea on the left. The moon is huddled in silver-lined clouds now, only peeping out now and then. I glance up at the cliffs. 'We've got bullet proof glass like Precious, haven't we, Monsieur?'

He looks at me quizzically. 'Precious? That's what you called my Bentley?'

I can't help grinning. 'Well, it was your favourite car, Monsieur.'

He laughs and this is only the third time I've ever heard Monsieur laugh. Then three things happen almost at once. There's a Smack as a spider's web with a round hole in it suddenly appears in the windscreen, and a gasp. And Monsieur is clutching his left shoulder.

'Monsieur, you're...'

'Faster, Joe!'

I ram my foot to the floor as another spider's web appears in the top right of the windscreen and my right ear stings. We round a corner and there is a load of blown up road, still smoking. The Bentley bumps along the verge only a few feet from the drop, as I fight to steer round the chaos. A third spider's web appears in the rear screen and there's a black hole in the roof lining. 'Monsieur!'

'Keep driving, Joe.' He's reaching beneath his seat with his good hand and opening a first aid pack. Pulling out a tourniquet.

Suddenly the sky blazes and the cliff on our right explodes in flames. The Bentley is thrown towards the cliff edge. I wrench the wheel and we're sliding sideways. Floor the throttle, stones flying as we regain the road. 'We're going to a hospital!'

He's tightening the tourniquet, his jaw set with pain. 'There is no safe refuge until we reach L'Étoile.'

'So I call Arnaud, yeah?'

He nods, trickles of sweat on his forehead.

'Joe?'

'Arnaud – where are you?'

'We will be landing at L'Étoile in five minutes. Is something wrong? I warned Father not to do this!'

'It's kept the heat off you people. But your dad's been shot, Arnaud. We need paramedics as soon as we get there.'

'Dear God, Joe. How far away are you?'

'We're just approaching Cannes.'

'What about the Cannes A and E hospital?'

'They'll have it staked out, just like all the others.'

'I will call the paramedics now.'

The sky whitens again; but this time the missile explodes just behind us, blowing in the Bentley's rear screen. I don't think our defence systems are in very good shape now. Monsieur's eyes are closed. 'Monsieur! You must stay awake!'

He whispers, 'I can hear you, Joe.'

A pencil beam rakes the cliffs to our right. The copter again. 'Can we shoot it down, Monsieur?'

His words come in quiet gasps. 'No need for such carnage… beneath your seat… aim… through the windscreen.'

It looks like a Magnum, but I guess it isn't. 'It takes out their comms?'

A slight nod, before his eyes close again. I wait until we've negotiated the next couple of hairpins and the moon is shining brightly on our prey. Then I see the copter starting to drop towards us. Someone's taking aim. Let's hope mine is better. Gripping the steering wheel with my left hand, I sight and squeeze the trigger in one movement with my right.

A brilliant laser beam joins us momentarily to the black bug in the sky. Then their cabin illuminates in a white light before going completely black. The searchlight has gone. And so, hopefully, have all their instruments, communications and weaponry. The last I see of the copter is this ungainly beetle making a wobbly descent to somewhere behind the cliffs.

My mobile goes. 'How is Father?' Over the hands free, Arnaud's voice is quiet with tension.

'Do not concern yourself, Arnaud. Joe will get us both home alive.'

I'll never know what it cost Monsieur to say that so steadily. As Arnaud ends the call, Monsieur's head falls back and his eyes close again. Sweat is pouring down his face; he's ashen white. He must be losing blood despite the tourniquet. Stamping on the throttle, I reach out and grab his hand. 'I'm not going to let you go, Monsieur! You're not going anywhere except home! D'you hear me?'

A slight nod. We take the next bend at eighty.

'It's you who've got to be pig-headed now, Monsieur. You're better at it even than me!'

The moon casts a stray beam into the cabin. Is that a trace of a half-smile? The Bentley's tail swings slightly wide as we come out of the bend. Feels like the rear tyres have some battle damage. But they're runflats – they can do this for another two hundred miles at least. I squeeze Monsieur's hand. It feels so cold. 'Don't leave me, Monsieur! Not you... not now... please!'

I drive the rest of that trip fuelled by high octane anger, nothing else. Like only my fury can keep hold of Monsieur. I almost hope we'll see another Aquila car again, just so that I can have the pleasure of shooting it into a blazing fireball. But mercifully the roads are now empty. Letting me drive as I've never done in my life.

—⁓—

Gravel flies as the Bentley roars up the drive to the blue flashing lights of the ambulance. Arnaud, Becks and Tommaso are waiting outside; I guess Talia is in the house, being cared for by Madame de L'Étang. Arnaud flings open the car door and watches, his face as white as his father's, as the paramedics get an oxygen mask onto Monsieur and do some quick checks. Then they rush him into the ambulance. Blue lights flashing, the ambulance kicks up more gravel as it heads out of the cast iron gates.

'Get in, Arnaud!'

He nods and opens the front passenger door. It's only then that we see how much blood Monsieur has lost. 'Father, what have they done to you!' Shaking his head in shock, his eyes bright with tears, Arnaud slams the door in a kind of fury.

Tommaso slides into the back seat with him. 'If I may come too? So much of this is my fault!'

Becks calls to us, 'I'll stay here with Talia and Madame!'

We tear after the ambulance. 'Where are they taking him, Arnaud?'

'It is a private clinic on the outskirts of Aix.'

'So, less chance of the wrong people knowing about it?'

'I hope so.' Arnaud turns to Tommaso and holds out his hand. 'I am sorry, Tommaso, not to have been able to greet you properly before. It is a privilege to meet Talia's brother.'

Tommaso's thin hand grasps Arnaud's. 'You fly a copter well, my friend.'

I catch his eye in the rear view mirror. 'Tommaso, what do you think... about the security in this clinic?'

'Show me where it is.'

Arnaud brings it up on his phone. 'Here, to the South West. Clinique St Marie des Hospitaliers.'

'Why this one, Arnaud?'

'When Father and I went to see Le Loup, he said that this was the hospital used by the network when someone was ill or injured because of its security and its discretion?'

Tommaso shakes his head. 'I have never heard anyone in the Camorra talk of it. So hopefully your father will be safe.'

CHAPTER 8

In the Garden

The place is more like a posh hotel than a hospital. We're sat in a waiting room with real coffee machines and even biscuits and pastries, which have a short life once I've spotted them. Arnaud prowls up and down, restless and haunted. Tommaso sits looking at his feet, hands clasped in front of him.

Arnaud looks at me. 'How can you eat like a pig at a time like this, Joe?'

'Easy. I'm starving hungry. An' if I don't eat like a pig, I won't be driving your dad's car very well next time I'm behind the wheel, will I?'

'Sorry.'

'Don't be sorry. Why not let me get you a latte? They're brilliant.'

In the end, I talk both of them into sitting down and grabbing coffee and pastries. And we watch Sky F1 on this HD TV. If I've learned one thing, it's that worrying is completely pointless unless you can work out a plan. And if you don't have enough information to work out a plan, you might as well eat pastries and drink latte and generally keep your strength up.

About six hours later, with sunlight flooding through the windows and the table between us completely covered with bits of pastry and biscuit, we're still wide awake. The F1 is long gone, as are Bond, QI, Attenborough and Wheeler Dealers but there's this episode of Top Gear where they race lorries and Clarkson's just has to catch fire. At this point, a really well-dressed dude who doesn't look at all like a surgeon cruises up to us. 'Which one of you is Arnaud, please?'

Arnaud jumps to his feet. 'Can I see my father now?'

The smart dude shakes his head. 'I am sorry, Arnaud, but your father is still on a life support system because of his huge loss of blood. He has had a transfusion and also an operation to remove the bullet from his shoulder. After the operation, he is still unconscious.'

Arnaud is so silent and he looks so strained that I sort of take over. 'What's the outlook? Is Monsieur going to live?'

The well-dressed dude loosens his tie and I notice that he's not shaved in days. Suddenly he looks human. 'Why, yes, of course.' He turns to Arnaud. 'Your father is physically in very good shape, Arnaud. It will take time but there is no reason why he should not make a full recovery.'

There are tears in Arnaud's dark eyes. 'Thank God. I thought...'

I put an arm round him. 'You're not going to lose your dad today, Arnaud.'

As I hug Arnaud, I see Tommaso's pale face looking at me, full of ghosts. And I remember Monsieur's words. *Talia's brother is bearing a terrible burden.*

—⁂—

The smart and very human dude says we can wait the two hours or so it will take for Monsieur to come round and some checks to be made. He sends for more pastries, although by this time my mouth's watering for a bacon butty. I look through the window at the gardens outside. 'Is it OK if we take a stroll?'

'Of course. The gardens are very beautiful at this time of year.' He opens French doors and the scent of some kind of flower washes over me so strongly, it makes me dizzy.

Tommaso takes my right arm. 'It is strong, the mimosa. Are you OK, Joe?'

'Yeah. I just thought… we've got a bit of time together now, us three. And like they say, it's good to talk?'

Arnaud comes to my left side and we three walk together on the soft grass in the early morning sunshine. In the trees, small birds call. A very large black and white cat, who reminds me of Fats, stalks around bushes and glares at us.

'This is Corbo's sort of place isn't it, Tommaso?'

'He would not like the cat!' A pause, then, 'You can ask me now, Joe Grayling. Now that my sister is safe – thanks to you all!'

I catch a glimpse of Arnaud's eyes and know, from his nod, that he and Monsieur have come at these same questions from another angle. Le Loup.

'Only if you want to tell us, Tommaso. There's so much that is very painful for you, isn't there?'

The thin face with its intense blue eyes looks beyond me. 'Was painful. Now, I have my sister. And I have friends.'

Arnaud says steadily, 'You will always have friends in us, Tommaso.'

Tommaso looks directly at Arnaud. 'You love Talia, don't you?'

Arnaud doesn't hesitate. 'Yes, I love Talia. Is that OK, Tommaso?'

That thin smile. 'It is very OK. I am so happy that she has you to care for her.'

Just up ahead is a small fountain, gushing out of a grey granite boulder. A bright green frog sits on top and I hope he's noticed the cat. We pause, the three of us, and Tommaso gazes at the sparkling water. 'I know all these things about you, Joe Grayling, because we share the same surname.' There's a pause, when all we can hear is the gently falling water. I hold my breath, waiting. Tommaso's voice is slow and tired. 'My father was your father's older brother.'

'My father had a *brother*?' And I'm hearing this word '*was*'...

'You would never have known about him. My father told me that, once, they were very close. They went to the same university and fought side by side in the SAS. They were in the network together. Then, my father said, someone made him an offer he could not refuse. Those were his words....'

'Who...?'

'The Contessa, my mother. Talia's mother.'

'Seventeen years ago?'

'My father said that he broke off all contact from that point.'

'When did he tell you this?'

'On the same night that he told me about my sister.'

'And then you ran away, to the Camorra?'

He nods. 'I never saw my father again. I didn't care. I was too angry with him.' His blue eyes challenge mine. 'I only found out he was dead by accident.'

'How... did he die?'

'The Contessa poisoned him... on the night of Talia's birthday party. The night that Talia herself came close to death.'

I'm looking at that stone room with its myriad candles, as I clutch my Napoleon hat; seeing the white uniformed figure of the masked chauffeur catching the dart in a gloved hand. And I'm hearing the Contessa's astonished, '*You!*'

'Your father had left, urgently, on the next stage of his mission. He had no idea that you and Becks were at that party and in extreme danger.'

'But your father knew?'

'Like I told you, the Camorra know everything. And my father knew more than most. Minutes after Commander Julius Grayling had left, my father slipped into impersonating his brother. It would not have been difficult – my father said, they were both accomplished spies and very alike in build. And he was simply taking up his old job again.'

'But why did he defy the Contessa to try and save us and Talia? If he and my father hadn't spoken for years…?'

'They loved each other as brothers, once. And I think my father regretted not having saved my sister, and made one last try.'

My head's spinning with the scent of mimosa. I'm remembering the chauffeur, all in white uniform, the sun blazing in his mirrored shades as he effortlessly swung Becks' huge suitcase into the boot of the white Mercedes. 'So, it was always your dad we saw… not mine?'

'It was always my father, Joe. He had been texting me for some time, trying to get me to come back to him. He said he would try anything to get Talia away from the Contessa. I thought it was all just empty promises and I never replied.'

Now I'm remembering the shock of seeing the dead man who looked like Dad and yet so not like him, and feeling horrified at how different he was from the photo. I'm hearing Monsieur's words. *I am afraid your father is much changed.*

Next thing, I'm leaning against a tree and the branches above are whirling around me. I struggle to make my mouth speak. But nothing comes out. Arnaud's voice is urgent. 'Joe – you have to get hold!' He grabs my shoulders.

Still nothing comes out. All I'm doing is shaking my head from side to side like some bewildered donkey. Dimly, I hear Tommaso's voice. 'Joe, it was a good thing that my father did for yours. It has made me able to love him again. And that is so much less painful than hating him!'

And the donkey replies, 'But he's dead!'

'Monsieur!' The unshaven, smartly dressed surgeon is hurrying across the grass, heading for Arnaud. 'Your father has regained consciousness.'

—∞—

It's a pleasant room where we find Monsieur, with French windows opening out onto the garden and the sound of birdsong. He's sitting up in bed, his left arm in a sling with huge padded bandages over his shoulder. Arnaud hugs him gently. 'You frightened us, Father!'

Monsieur's grey eyes are hawk-like, searching me and Tommaso, despite the pain he must be in. 'Have you two spoken?'

Tommaso replies quietly, 'I have told Joe that it was my father – his father's brother – who was killed by the Contessa.'

'That was brave of you, Tommaso. Please, sit down. I can see you are very tired.' Monsieur turns to me. 'This is a huge shock to you, I know, Joe. Julius never even hinted to me that he had a brother. But... when his brother had become his enemy...'

'And my dad is alive?'

Tommaso's voice is dull. 'Your father is in terrible danger, Joe. When you and Becks came after me in the woods, those men were gone because your father had given himself up to them.'

They have the one they wanted above all. '… WHY?'

'He was near to bringing down the biggest illegal arms warlord in the business, name of Aquila.'

'The one with the machine gun?'

Tommaso nods. 'Then, he discovered who Aquila's hostages were.'

My head aches. Ages ago, I'd given up hoping that Dad's path and mine would ever cross again. And now… 'I've got to get Dad out!'

'Joe, this is where you absolutely must listen to Tommaso!'

'I will be at your side, Joe. But there is much to find out before we can make a move.' Tommaso looks all in. I hesitate. Instantly, the blue eyes challenge mine. 'What is it you want to know?'

'How did you discover how your dad died?'

'When I found the contact details for Zeitgeist in the Camorra office, I called him to warn him that there was a contract out for him. We met in secret. He and this other agent…' He looks at Monsieur.

'Le Loup. They both knew what had happened. But as I had been out of the network for some time, the word would not have come to me.'

'And your dad was a double agent in the network. He was the one who'd set up Zeitgeist?'

Tommaso's voice is very tired. 'I think you can guess his codename, Joe.'

The glittering ruby stick twirls in front of my eyes as I remember my father's mission for a certain agent who might know about the twins. 'Michelangelo?'

Tommaso's face is strained, dark shadows beneath his eyes. 'So you see, Joe, my father was what was wrong in the network.'

'Tommaso.' Monsieur's voice is gentle but firm. 'You must stop reproaching yourself for your father's mistakes. In the end, he paid the highest price for his courage.' He holds out his hand.

Slowly, Tommaso takes Monsieur's hand in both of his. 'Thank you, Monsieur!'

I find myself murmuring, 'Ammo that can blast through bullet proof glass…'

Arnaud's voice is very quiet. 'I also will be at your side, Joe. It was Aquila who shot my father.'

—⁂—

After Arnaud and Tommaso have gone to get the Bentley I'm about to follow them, when a flash of silver from the mantelpiece catches my eye. I pick up the slim, bright bullet and turn it in the light. 'This is what nearly killed you, Monsieur?'

The half-smile. 'It would certainly have killed me if you had not won that argument, Joe.'

'How did it get through bullet proof glass?'

'Not so much how did it get through two inches of reinforced glass – because most bullets will do that. But how did it continue to travel at a velocity sufficient to do such damage?'

'So was he at close range?'

'At the roadside, most probably. But Aquila has also developed ultra high-velocity rifles.'

I'm back in that cabin in the forest with Becks, splinters of wood flying as the man in the Mac lets off steam. 'Stetson. Spurs and not the footie club. A bit irritable?'

'Then you have met Aquila.'

'Talks like he's taking tea at Harrods?'

'And has killed more than three hundred times at the last count.'

'What's his thing then?'

Monsieur takes the bullet from me and looks at it thoughtfully. 'Aquila is an arms dealer on the largest imaginable scale. He has been behind all the bloodiest coups and revolutions that have taken place in the third world over the last ten years. He supplies the Camorra and all the major drugs gangs fund him. They live in fear of him because his army of mercenaries is the deadliest there is.'

'So Tommaso…?'

'Will have been aware of this man ever since he joined the Camorra.'

'And he could know even more about Stetson than Dad?'

'It is very possible. You must let yourselves be guided by Tommaso.'

'I guess he'll tell Talia about… everything… in his own time?'

Monsieur nods. 'He will know how and when.' A breeze begins to blow in from the garden, moving the curtains. The birdsong hushes. Before I take my leave of Monsieur, I quietly close the French doors.

—∞—

Inside the Bentley, the bloodstains have been carefully cleaned up by this very discreet hospital that the Camorra don't know about. The rear end's been quite a bit modified by the missile damage. But the tyres will see us home. As I get behind the wheel, Arnaud in the front passenger seat, Tommaso is reaching for something on the floor behind us. He holds up the small, deadly piece of metal; the same as the one on the mantelpiece in Monsieur's room. 'Aquila's calling card.' He slips the bullet into the pocket where he keeps his knife.

CHAPTER 9

The Sixth Co-ordinate

'This is going to be completely random, you do know that, don't you?' Becks' fingers fly across the keys with the password, the ruby stick flashes fire and the screen fills with the first directory. She clicks on Properties. 'OK, this stick is 64 gig. Are we sure that we've looked at everything that's showing here?'

I look at Becks, rubbing my eyes. 'Well, are we? I'm seeing double after all these goes through the files.'

She stares at the directory, running a hand through a twirl of red hair. 'Why don't we assume that what's accessible is nothing like as important as what isn't?'

In a tone of slight interest, Tommaso says, 'You mean, deleted files?'

'Yeah.'

'Definitely! There could also be hidden files that are individually password protected.'

Arnaud frowns. 'Both of these file categories are not accessible through the Windows operating system, are they?'

Becks shakes her head. 'They need a clever little program to be written. By someone who really knows what they're doing. And that person isn't me.'

Tommaso brushes lanky blond hair from his eyes. He looks a whole load better. Since getting back to L'Étoile, we've all showered, food is on the way and Arnaud has given Tommaso a slick set of black jeans and tops. 'I could maybe help you, Becks. I got some experience with computer programming in my last job.'

A slow smile gleams in Becks' green eyes. She drags up a chair. 'Let's go, Tommaso!'

Arnaud looks at me and shrugs. 'Are we redundant, Joe?'

'Nope. You and I have some phone calls to make, Arnaud. We have a team to build, yeah?'

We go into the library where I call Lenny and get his voicemail, as succinct as ever: 'Lenny, fitness trainer. Sorry. Try later?'

'He'll still be at work.' I leave a voicemail for him.

Arnaud has better luck with Michel. 'Comment ça va Michel? Oui, oui… très bien. Il s'agit d'une petite affaire comme celle en la Corse. Je ne connais pas encore les détails, mais on aura besoin de toi, mon ami.'

He listens then punches the air. 'Michel is in!'

'So we're five. Hoping on six.'

Arnaud paces the room. 'If we just knew the location, we could make preparations.'

'Well, those two-way radios and seriously good torches were pretty useful in Corsica. Have you got them here?'

'Of course!' Arnaud is heading for the library door when it opens. Talia stands there in her pyjamas, a bemused smile on her face. 'What is going on? You are all so busy!'

Madame de L'Étang is immediately at her side, fluffy white dressing gown in hand. 'Ma chérie, il fait froid! Et tu dois te détendre.'

'Dear Madame, I have slept so well and I have taken all those disgusting pills from the hospital – please don't worry yourself!'

Talia lets Madame wrap the dressing gown around her and sits reluctantly on the settee while Madame disappears in search of hot choc. There's a steely look in those bright blue eyes. 'Now, Joe and Arnaud – who is going to tell me what is going on here?'

Arnaud sits down next to her. Gently taking her hand, he recounts all that has happened since Monsieur's helicopter brought her safely to L'Étoile. He only talks to her about Monsieur, not my dad and not her and Tommaso's. And there is nothing about the deadly exchange outside the cave; I'm relieved that Arnaud instinctively seems to understand the message that only Tommaso can give to his sister. Talia goes very quiet. When she looks up, her face is sombre. 'Monsieur... is he going to live?'

'Yes, Talia, but it will take time for him to get his

strength back. I want you to be here for him. Dear Madame is not as young as she was.'

'Of course!' Talia catches Arnaud in a hug. 'I will be proud to care for your father, Arnaud.' Her face falls slightly. 'And I know that I would be useless on your mission, although I wish so much I could come!'

He strokes her hair. 'You and my father are the two most precious souls on earth to me. It makes me happy to think that you will be safe here together.' Madame appears with the hot choc and isn't going to take any argument. She shepherds Talia upstairs.

Seconds later, Becks bursts breathlessly into the room. 'We've got something – Tommaso's cracked the deleted files!' We all pile next door. The light from the screen glows on Tommaso's thin face and his eyes shine as he shows us a directory that Becks and I have never seen before. It's labelled '*Obtained from a man in a hat*'. Slightly shocked that Dad could actually joke about the casually murderous Aquila, I stare at the small column of six files. 'How on earth did you do it, Tommaso?'

He swivels his chair and takes me in with his young/old face. 'I learned a great deal from watching my father hack into the network.' Becks and I exchange looks. Quick as a flash, Tommaso asks, 'What is it?'

'Someone hacked into our network here and was sending emails to Talia's address, claiming to be her father.'

Tommaso stares at Becks. 'When?'

'In the last few days – so it couldn't have been your father, Tommaso.'

His eyes have a dull anger. 'No. Not my father. But the one we met on the mountain.'

I remember Aquila touching Becks' hair and her kick that made him recoil. *Get stuffed, perv.* I find I'm saying this out loud.

'Yes, Joe. He likes young girls. Why do you think I was so desperate to get Talia out of there?'

'So it was Aquila sending the emails?'

His voice is scornful. 'Not him personally. But he would have got the best hackers on the case. He likes playing games.'

Becks' voice is full of disgust. 'Well we're not playing his!' Then her voice changes. 'Except, we might have to make him think we are.'

And if I'd just listened to what Becks was saying, I might have been that bit quicker off the mark not long after. But the donkey stares at the screen. 'I can't make out these file names. Can you open them?'

Becks double clicks. 'You can… but this is what you get.'

We stare at the blank screen. 'Are they all like this?'

'Every single one. At first we thought the contents had been hidden in some way, but Tommaso's been all through them and they really are just empty files.'

'There is just one possibility that we haven't looked at.' Tommaso speaks cautiously. 'It is a technique used a lot in the Camorra.'

Becks looks at him closely. 'What's that?'

'The thing of significance is not the contents of the file but its name.'

We all gaze at the column of files. They all look similar, somehow. The first one goes: 43x53f52ez, the next 3x50f42ez

Arnaud points, 'There is some kind of pattern of letters and numbers. Also, the letters seem to start in the middle of the alphabet and then pick up letters from either end, but this pattern is far from clear.'

'Suppose we remove these troublesome letters.' Tommaso scribbles rapidly on a sheet of paper. 'Does this remind you of anything?'

43 _ 53 _ 52_ _

'A phone number?'

Becks frowns. 'It's the right number of characters. But it doesn't start with zero.'

Tommaso whispers, 'Joe, show us what you input to your phone to establish the sat nav position of L'Étoile.'

As I tap the keys, it slowly dawns on all of us. 'Of course! If you substitute the first letter for the degree symbol, the second for the minutes and the third and fourth for the seconds, each file name is a co-ordinate!'

'Tommaso, you're a genius!'

He shakes his head at Becks. 'We MUST identify quickly where these places are!'

The computer suddenly decides to slow down to a snail's pace so we all reach for our phones. Becks gets in first. 'The top two are in the mountains above Rome – the hut where Aquila ambushed us and the cave where we found Talia.'

'I suppose that's how Dad was able to track down the gang…'

The computer wakes up under Tommaso's impatient fingers. The Google Maps screen changes to a remote coastline with islands dotted around a headland. Becks points, 'The Scottish Highlands; the third co-ord is Kyle of Lochalsh, a small fishing town opposite the Isle of Skye.'

Arnaud comments, 'Very picturesque – but what could be the significance?'

Tommaso shakes his head, 'That we have to discover. The fourth co-ordinate is even more puzzling; it's out at sea, about ten miles off the mainland, Northwest of the fishing town.'

Becks taps a pen against her teeth. 'So what is the perv planning up there? And could that be where they're taking your dad, Joe?'

'If he's still alive…'

'STOP being negative!'

'The fifth co-ordinate,' Tommaso taps on the keyboard, 'is even more strange.' The scene on the screen zooms in on the coast of Africa, to a part of the Belgian Congo.

Arnaud says, 'Maybe this one is not so obscure. The Belgian Congo has been the arena for many bloody uprisings in recent years, where the use of mercenaries and imported arms has brought massive loss of life to the local people.'

Becks nods, 'So this seems to have the perv's

smelly fingers all over it – he's planning to sell arms to Africa. Your dad must have got wise to Aquila's next move, Joe.'

I don't answer. I'm looking from my phone where I tapped in the co-ords for the chateau, to the last file name on the list. 'Aquila's got L'Étoile in his sights too.'

—⚌—

There's complete silence in the room as we stare at the sixth co-ordinate. Everyone jumps as my mobile goes. 'Monsieur?'

'We have to be brief, Joe, for reasons that you will understand. You must leave for a northern location. Le Loup says that you should be able to decode the co-ordinates.'

'We've got them, Monsieur.'

'Do you have a team?'

'Five, and hoping for six.'

'Six is a good number. Now please pass me to Arnaud, I need to talk to him about flight logistics.'

Tommaso brings up the Scottish fishing town on Google Maps and we gaze at the wild scenery and the white bridge that soars from the mainland to the Isle of Skye. Arnaud waves me over. 'Can Lenny get to Marlingford? It's a small private airfield south west of Bristol where we can refuel and pick him up.'

'I'll check – but take it that he can.'

While Arnaud continues to talk with his father,

Tommaso zooms in further on the coastal waters round the headland.

'It is very beautiful.' Talia gazes at the white-tipped waves. She must have crept quietly in, evading Madame.

Tommaso takes her hand but he's frowning. 'And, I suspect, very dangerous in more ways than one.'

'Why so, my brother?' Time-worn boy and fragile girl look eye to eye at each other; and I wonder what it must feel like for the twins to be together at last after those seventeen lost years.

Tommaso zooms out to a view of the whole of Scotland. 'Some years ago, the Italian police were becoming better at their job, so the Camorra moved into Aberdeen.'

'They came to *Scotland*?' Becks and I exchange looks, and I'm not sure this is on her A-Level History curriculum.

'They have been highly successful there because the Scottish police are not used to this form of crime, which can cover itself so easily with a cloak of respectability.'

Becks twirls a lock of red hair round and round her index finger. 'So the perv won't be short of mates, will he?'

Arnaud comes off his phone. 'I have warned father about the sixth co-ordinate. He did not seem surprised. Apparently, there is a contingency plan.'

I wonder if what's left of the Bentley gunship has anything to do with this contingency plan. I can't help seeing all that blood. And, despite my desperation to see Dad again, hug him and bring him home, I begin to ask myself if I should be trying to do this.

—∞—

Madame de L'Étang calls us into the dining room to eat and we fall on the beef stew until we're completely stuffed. Even Talia has a decent helping and Becks goes for seconds. I'll never know how she stays so slim. Must be the kick boxing. Just as I'm thinking this very thought, my phone goes.

'Joe?'

'Lenny! It's so good to hear from you!'

'S'good. Things OK?'

I explain how not OK they are and how I need his help.

'Like Corsica, yeah?'

'Only a lot harder.'

'Michel along?'

'He's up for it, and another mate too.'

'Where you wanna meet?'

Becks is jumping up and down to get my attention. I nod at her and she gives a whoop. 'We got Lenny! Whooh!'

'Becks says Hi. Now, d'you know of this airstrip called Marlingford, not far from Bristol – we can pick you up there? I'll text you the time.'

Lenny knows how to get there. 'S'y later Joe.'

Planning for an early start, we all go upstairs to grab a few hours sleep. As Arnaud turns at the top of the stairs, I ask him, 'Is Michel coming here or…'

'He is well on his way. Dors bien, Joe.'

I fall into an exhausted sleep, invaded by some strange dreams, and wake to hear a raucous cawing on my balcony. The rising sun sends pale rainbows through the stained glass windows onto the walls. Yawning, I fall out of bed and open the French doors. Corbo flaps his wings, looking pleased with himself. On the balcony rail is a dead mouse minus its head. 'Is that for me?'

He caws again as Becks opens her French windows and pads outside in jeans and T-shirt, rubbing sleepy eyes. 'I might have known, you noisy bird!' She looks down at the garden. 'Hey, Joe – Michel's arrived!'

A white horse is grazing peacefully, tethered to a bush; Mistral looks up with dark, bright eyes, ears pricked forward and snorts softly. Becks and I tiptoe downstairs and find a sleeping Michel in the lounge, his black Guardien cloak draped over him, boots on the floor, saddle and bridle flung over a chair. His eyes slowly open and he smiles. With his shoulder length dark hair, he could be Arnaud's brother; quite apart from having a shared childhood with Arnaud after his dad died. Becks whispers, 'Chill Michel – we'll get you a café au lait.' He nods and closes his eyes again.

Half an hour later, all six of us are sat round a loaded breakfast table with Madame presiding over a steaming coffee pot and foaming hot milk. Talia is helping her, looking much brighter than last night. I grab my fourth croissant. 'Did you manage to track down the two way radios and the torches, Arnaud?'

'And some spare batteries. But I think we might need more than three radios.'

Becks spreads honey onto her pain au chocolat. 'It's a huge climbing area up there. You've got Ben Nevis for goodness sake – I've been Googling it. I bet we can buy more radios if we swing by Fort William.'

'How do we swing by Fort William in a helicopter?'

Becks gives me a strange look. 'The, er, Fort William heliport?'

'Alright, Miss Clever, just pass me the honey, yeah?'

—m—

When Madame starts clearing the plates, having smilingly refused all help from Becks and Talia, I go walking. Those disturbing dreams from last night are on my mind and I need someone to give me some straight advice.

In the field behind the chateau, Arnaud and Michel are loading tents and sleeping bags into the copter. I go looking for Tommaso. But then I see him walking hand in hand with Talia in a shady copse, in quiet conversation. And I guess that he's telling her all those painful things about their father, so I turn quickly away.

Back in the chateau's dining room, sitting at the table with the computer and the ruby memory stick, I phone Monsieur. 'I'm really sorry to trouble you, Monsieur. How are you doing?'

His voice is stronger than yesterday. 'I hoped you would call, Joe. If not, I was going to call you. This is extremely difficult for you, isn't it?'

'I'm having problems believing that Dad is alive, Monsieur.'

'Completely understandable. When you thought you saw your dead father, it must have been shocking to see him so changed, but you had to adjust to it. Now, there is another shocking adjustment to be made.'

'So... you believe Dad's alive?'

'It was a relief to know that the man we saw lying dead was not your father, Joe. But it was a great grief to know that it was his brother, however estranged they had become.'

'But... now that Dad's handed himself over to Aquila... what are his chances?'

'Think like your enemy, Joe. What do you think is in Aquila's mind at this moment?'

I stare at the glittering fire of the memory stick. 'I guess he'll be expecting a rescue attempt... but most likely from the network, not us.'

'Exactly so.'

'So he won't be expecting a bunch of teenagers.'

'You will need to look like impoverished students, probably on a camping trip. I suggest that you do not go around publicly in a band of six. Three by three or four by two will blend in less noticeably.'

I'm still feeling more and more like the donkey. 'Monsieur – how on earth am I going to get Dad back?'

'That depends on your information, Joe. And you won't know what you have until you have thoroughly checked out the fourth co-ordinate.'

'The one in the waters off the Scottish coast? Does the network know what it is, Monsieur?'

'It is completely unknown to Le Loup.'

'But… I shouldn't be risking my mates' lives like this, should I?'

'They do not see it like that, Joe. With your combined experience and cool heads, you are all commandos now.'

'So… you don't think it's a mission impossible?'

Monsieur's voice is very calm. 'If I thought that it was impossible, Joe, I would never allow you to go. It will be an extraordinary mission, fraught with unexpected dangers and obstacles. But I believe that you and your friends – especially Tommaso – have a better chance than anyone of bringing your father home alive.'

CHAPTER 10

An Extraordinary Mission

Out in the field by the chateau, the rotors of the black copter turn slowly as our feet swish through the long grass. There's a rhythmic thudding behind us. Michel swings off Mistral's bare back and gives Monsieur's beloved horse a hug. 'Vas-y, mon ami!' Mistral lowers himself and rolls in the grass, kicking his hooves in the air. Then he gets to his feet, shakes himself all over and plunges his head into the clover like his life depends on it. Michel sprints to the copter.

Ahead of me and Becks, Corbo has decided to hitch a ride on Tommaso's shoulder. 'Is he coming with?'

He shakes his head. 'Just a goodbye. For a crow, he's very sentimental.' Again, I get that startling flashback to the way Dad used to say things. And I wish I'd known Dad's brother, my uncle Sebastian; even though Michelangelo was the crack in the network, he did something amazing in the end.

Chuckling loudly, Corbo nibbles at Tommaso's

ear in a way that looks painful. Then he beats those mighty wings and lifts off, wheeling away to the thin top branch of a lightning-blasted tree. Tommaso watches the dark bird and seems to make the very slightest nod in Corbo's direction. Then he runs to the copter and pulls himself up and inside.

My eyes are caught by Becks' bulging handbag. 'What's in that?'

She dodges out of reach. 'NTK.'

'What?'

'Need to know.'

'I do need to know.'

She pats the handbag. 'You'll all be glad I brought… them.'

The rotor blades start to turn faster and we hurry to the cabin, the down draft turning Becks' hair into a small whirlwind.

At the controls, Arnaud frowns. 'This is not an old ladies' picnic for goodness sake! Get in and put your belts on!' Tommaso is sitting next to him, adjusting sat nav and radar like he's done this before. And I guess that garbage trucks and getaway cars weren't the only vehicles the Camorra got him to drive.

Michel leans forward from the rear seats, waving his mobile. 'Lenny est en route à Marlingford.'

I slam shut the sliding door, the rotors thunder and the long grass flattens as we leave the ground on a forward tilt and gather speed. In the field, Mistral rears, white mane and tail streaming, as we head for the sky and the Northwest.

The flight to England is mostly masked in sleep for me. From time to time, I wake up and see Arnaud in conversation with Tommaso but they both seem to know exactly what they're doing, so I doze off again. When I next wake up, I catch glimpses of the sea through gaps in the cloud. I glance across at Becks and she's looking downwards too. She smiles sleepily, and closes her eyes again. And I feel suddenly terrified at what I'm leading Becks into, when I should be trying to get her as far away from the perv in the Stetson as possible. When I dream again, all I can see is the bullets and dust flying as he blasts his way out of that hut to make it crush us to death. All I can feel is the earth moving beneath us, while those express trains of the quakes roar ceaselessly all around.

I wake up, vision blurred. We seem to be in a thick fog that billows past the windows. My stomach lurches as the copter tilts. 'What's going on?'

Arnaud's voice is relaxed. 'Just a descent through low cloud, Joe.'

'Will you teach me to fly this machine, Arnaud?'

'Of course. I learned in one week with my father.'

'And are you, like, legal? I mean, what age…?'

'Just as legal as you are in the Bentley, Joe.'

We're through the clouds and heading for this small aerodrome with green hills beyond. In his impeccable English, Arnaud radios the control tower and gets permission to land. A few gliders are parked outside three huge aircraft hangars, as the copter heads towards a refuelling station and slowly drops to the ground.

Tommaso's eyes scan the airfield. 'I don't like this – too quiet.' Apart from a few pigeons on the hangar roofs, nothing moves. And there's no sign of Lenny. Becks calls him. After a few seconds, her face strained, she puts their conversation on speaker. Lenny's voice is tight as a wire. 'You got fuel to get to 'nother place?'

Arnaud replies, 'Half an hour.'

'Go. An' encrypt all messages!'

Becks looks at us. 'He's switched off his phone. We must be under surveillance.'

I stare across the innocent-looking airfield. 'I should have known! Let's get out of here, Arnaud.' The rotors roar like multiple machine guns as Arnaud rams the controls into a full power climb.

As the helicopter lifts into the air again, Tommaso and I send an encrypted text message to Monsieur with questions about the nearest refuelling point. He gets back to us, and we relay the data to Lenny. Lenny has to drive twenty three miles north of Bristol. His message comes back: 'M5 clear – 20 minutes.'

Arnaud's voice is urgent. 'Where is this airfield? We are getting very low on fuel!'

'It's five minutes for us, Arnaud. Staverton. Near Cheltenham.'

'Give me one reason why Staverton, near

Cheltenham, is safer than your Marlingford, near Bristol!'

Becks shouts above the roar of the rotors, 'Lenny saw a helicopter gunship hovering above a field behind Marlingford!'

'Hell...!' We thunder towards the low cloud ceiling. 'And do the Camorra know about Staverton?'

'They don't know we're going there. There are nearer refuelling points, so they're going to have to guess.'

Tommaso nods at Becks, who sends an encrypted message to Lenny to confirm the new pickup point. In the back, Michel's keen eyes scan the skies as we emerge above the cloud. Tommaso checks the radar. 'They must have been preparing to open fire when we took off... on the ground, we would have been completely helpless.'

'But they can track us on their radar, can't they?'

'We are faster and more manoeuvrable than them. We must aim to get out of their range before we set course for Staverton.'

Arnaud explodes. 'But that is going to use yet more fuel!'

'It is vital if we are to give them the slip.'

Swearing under his breath, Arnaud flicks anxious glances at the fuel gauge and the radar as we hurtle along just above the cloud. After a nerve-wracking five minutes, Tommaso turns to Arnaud. 'We have lost them. Here is your course for Staverton...'

As we swing round, I whisper to Becks, 'The

problem is going to be the time it takes Lenny to get there…'

She nods. 'Time for our friends with guns to make a lucky guess.'

—◊—

After we change course, it takes only around five minutes to reach Staverton but it feels like five hours. This place is bigger and much busier than Marlingford. We have to wait for a Lear jet to take off before we can descend, with more nail-biting minutes watching the rock bottom fuel gauge. But at least there's a security guard waiting for us by the refuelling station and a mechanic to give us a hand with refilling the tank.

Becks whispers, 'Arnaud's getting some curious looks from those dudes – d'you think they're wondering about his age?'

'He can easily pass for older with his height.'

'And I s'pose with that long dark hair and black jeans, he could be a rock star with his own private copter?'

'So let's try and look like part of his team.' I rummage in my camping bag and find the sunglasses I wore in the Bentley.

Becks gives me a despairing look. 'You are ridiculous!'

Arnaud is following the security guard into an office on the edge of the airfield to pay for the fuel, when I catch sight of Michel and Tommaso staring at a distant figure sprinting towards us. Becks has seen it too. 'Lenny! Brilliant!'

But now Tommaso's eyes are looking in another direction. Following his gaze, I see sunlight glinting on something in the far distance. He hurries over to me and Becks. 'Someone is watching us with binoculars. We had better be prepared to get out of here fast. I will warn Arnaud.'

Seconds later, Lenny is with us, barely out of breath, his boxer's face with a broad grin. We all shake. 'That gym instructor job of yours must keep you fit, mate!'

'S'good, Joe.' With Lenny's usual abbreviated style, I'm not clear whether he's saying the job's good or it's good to see us; probably he means both.

We turn to see Arnaud and Tommaso running across from the office; Arnaud's voice is urgent. 'Go!'

We hurl ourselves back into the copter, the rotors roar and less than a minute later we're airborne again. Looking down, I can still see that flash of sunlight on glass. Tommaso is looking too, until it disappears. For a couple of minutes he taps into his phone, then turns to Arnaud. 'There is a heliport at Kyle of Lochalsh. I know we were going to land at Fort William to get more radios, but...'

'You are right, Tommaso. There is no time to be lost – three will have to be sufficient.'

'I guess we will have to refuel once more?'

Arnaud nods. 'Our range is 485 nautical miles and the distance to Fort William is 475 miles. That did not leave us enough of a margin, so my father contacted a small airfield South of Glasgow.'

Tommaso taps into his phone again. 'Kyle of Lochalsh is 525 miles from Staverton.'

'So, flying at 195mph, and allowing for the refuel, we should be there in about three hours. Can you contact my father for him to arrange things?'

After I've spoken to Monsieur, it takes more than an hour to update Lenny and Michel with the many twists and turns of a story that began more than seventeen years ago.

—m—

The second refuelling stop near Glasgow passes off with none of the scares of the first one. And now the four of us passengers behind the pilot and co-pilot are looking down at the scenery with a growing interest. On the horizon are the outlines of craggy peaks that soar like an ancient wall above the gently rolling hills that lead towards them. As we get closer, we can see more and more peaks stretching into the distance. The nearer ones have streaks of grey and purple clouds trailing below the summits. Silver streams run down the dark rock like tinsel; and on top of the highest peaks, patches of snow gleam white in the summer sun.

Becks looks round at Lenny and Michel. 'Like Corsica, only a lot bigger?'

They nod, gazing in fascination at a land that is so utterly different from overcrowded England.

Very few roads weave between the mountains. There are no motorways; I can't imagine trying to build a motorway through this wild terrain. Then suddenly, we're flying over a vast stretch of glittering water flanked by mountains with pine trees on their lower slopes.

Becks is consulting her smartphone. 'It's a loch but I'm not sure which one. There's loads of them.'

Michel murmurs, 'Beautiful water.' Quite a compliment, when he's so in love with his native Camargue.

Lenny nods. 'Yeah.'

This dreamlike flight continues with no end to the mountain ranges and Michel's beautiful water. About half an hour into the Highlands, Tommaso turns to Arnaud. 'We have a good fuel supply and still two hours of light. Do you want to check out the fourth co-ordinate before we land?'

'Does the team?'

We're all up for it.

—⁂—

It's stunning, seeing the white Skye Bridge soaring across to the island for real instead of on a computer screen. The small lighthouse nestles just before the bridge on the right. As our copter sails above Kyle of Lochalsh, we look down on this small coastal town set between breathtaking mountains and the ocean. Small clusters of fishing boats are anchored in the harbour. Tommaso studies the sat nav closely as we bear right along the coastline before heading out to sea. The sky is almost free of cloud and the sun shines brightly on the water; the waves are moving choppily in what looks like a stiff wind. Apart from a small dinghy making heavy going on its way back to shore, there's absolutely nothing in sight.

Tommaso looks at Arnaud. 'We are exactly on the fourth co-ordinate.'

Arnaud puts the copter into hover. 'Is there nothing on the radar?'

'Nothing except for the little boat.'

'Then I'm going down as far as I can.'

As we drop further and further towards the restless waves, we all strain to see. 'Michel – you've got amazing eyesight. Surely you can spot something?'

He shakes his head. 'Rien du tout, Joe.'

We're now only about a hundred feet above the sea and strong gusts are rocking the copter. Arnaud starts to climb again. 'It's no good – the fourth co-ordinate is a bad joke!'

Beck says thoughtfully, 'Unless… could it be *under* the sea?'

'We'd need a boat with sonar to check that out, Becks.'

'That could be feasible. But my worry is that all this isn't finding your dad, Joe.'

'Monsieur felt that, if we could find the fourth co-ordinate, we'd have some clue about where Dad might be being held.'

'But with every minute and every hour that go past…'

'I know, I know… I just think that Monsieur's right, that's all. What do you think, Tommaso?'

He turns to me, his old/young eyes less tired than before. 'Aquila will utilise your father to do maximum damage to the network, so he will not be in a hurry to kill him.'

'But he'll torture him, won't he?'

Tommaso says quietly, 'Not yet. He likes to play with his prey.'

'Monsieur said he'll be expecting a rescue attempt. But not from us.'

'We must still be very careful, Joe.'

Right at that moment my phone goes. 'Monsieur?'

'You are on your way to the Kyle of Lochalsh heliport, Joe?'

'Nearly there.' I don't say anything about the fourth co-ordinate because we're not done with it yet.

'You are booked in to land, but I had to be somewhat creative to account for your youth and the fact that you are arriving with camping equipment.'

'What's the storyline, Monsieur?'

'You are working for a French film maker, reconnoitring and researching the area around Kyle of Lochalsh to make a new movie about the life of Rob Roy.'

'Rob…?'

'A kind of Scottish Robin Hood of the 18th

Century. Do not worry about the detail. Rob Roy is still revered in the Highlands. And for hundreds of years the Scots have had strong ties with France.'

'Right. And the camping gear is because we're, like, living rough like he did as a lot of the time he was on the run… like Robin Hood?'

'Your sense of history is impeccable, Joe.'

—⸎—

'I hate to say this but are we nearly there yet?' Becks heaves her bag higher onto her back as we trudge along a road brightly lit by our powerful Corsican torches. It must be an hour since we left the Kyle of Lochalsh heliport with our camping gear. I did wonder a bit about the story that Monsieur had concocted when the check-in lady asked Arnaud for his autograph. With a flourish and a smile, he scribbled an imagined name and he still won't tell us what it was.

I consult my phone's satnav, which keeps arguing with Arnaud's. 'It says, half a mile.'

'Truck!' Lenny calls from the rear. There's a dim roar about half a mile away. It won't be long; the last one nearly blew us into the ditch. We all shuffle onto the grass, through the ditch and into the hedge to avoid the monster.

After it's blasted past, Lenny trots on in front with Michel. Arnaud looks at his phone. 'The camping site we're looking for is called…' he shakes his head, 'no, I refuse to try and pronounce this!'

I venture, 'Afternaughty'?

Becks giggles helplessly. 'After naughty you get a detention!'

'Thanks Becks.'

Then we hear Lenny's voice again. 'Sign!'

At least Arnaud's and my phones agree about the name of the camping site and so does the sign: 'Auchternochty'. But after we take the turn, there's still more than a mile of mud-pitted track. When we finally arrive it's gone ten and there are no lights on in any of the tents. I suppose with no TV or computer games there's nothing else to do but call it a day.

We find a spot a good way off from the others, because we all know that what's going to happen next could be noisy. And so begins the great saga of The Putting Up of the Tents in the Dark. Episode One is Not Knowing our Ground Sheet from our Outer Tent. Two is Trying to Find the Inner Tent without Swearing. Three is The Losing of the Tent Poles in the Grass and Swearing Quietly. And Four is Me and Arnaud and Tommaso Getting Hopelessly Entangled Trying to Raise the Tent and Swearing Loudly while Lenny and Michel laugh uncontrollably.

Then a voice says sweetly, 'Would you like a hand?' With military precision, Becks dishes out orders and our tent is up in less than five minutes. Exhausted, the guys crawl inside and grab sleeping bags.

I wipe sweat from my forehead. 'So, where were

you?' She shines her torch to where her tent is, looking immaculate, about ten feet away. 'You did that on your own?'

'Well, mine is smaller, Joe. And I did D of E Bronze. A lot of it was about getting tents up quick and not losing things or people.'

'You never told me about that.'

'You never asked. You were doing footie those weekends, anyway.'

'OK, OK. But answer me this, because I might die of hunger otherwise. What is in your bag?'

'Are the others still awake?'

'Nah, they're knackered. Leave your bag to me, Becks.'

'Don't be so greedy!' She fishes inside this huge bag and very slowly prises the top off a bottle of Coke. Before the hiss of bubbles has finished, everyone is back outside the tent, eyes on the Becks bag. Passing round Coke bottles and Mars bars, she gives another of those sweet smiles. 'The condition, guys, is YOU buy the next meal. Whenever that might be.' Then Becks slides regally into her tent and we crawl back into ours.

—ᴍ—

I wake once in the night, and become instantly aware of what you share with four other dudes in a not very big tent. This includes the stench of sweat, the farting, the snoring and the sudden unexpected movement of limbs, like a kick up your backside or a high five delivered straight to your face. But at least I'm not cold, which is the only memory I have of camping on the school Geography expedition in the Brecon Beacons.

When I wake up next, the sun hasn't yet made the horizon. I look at my watch. Five thirty. I'm the only one left in the tent and it still smells poisonous. I pin back the tent door flaps to get some ventilation going.

'Joe! Come on!' Becks has an almost empty bag on her back. Lenny and Michel are tipping our rubbish into the camping site bins. Arnaud and Tommaso are shoving new batteries into the two-way radios. And the campsite dude is making his way towards us. I grab my wallet.

He's a young guy, friendly. 'How long yous guys plannin' on staying here?'

'Maybe a week. How much would that be?'

'For two tents, normally, that would be fifty quid. But as yous're doin' a movie about Bonnie Rob, then it's twenty five, man.'

Wondering at how fast news spreads in the Highlands, I fish out the cash from the remains of what Monsieur gave me and Becks all those months ago at L'Étoile. 'That's really good of you. We're just, like, taking a look, y'know?'

He grins. 'Sure. Enjoy!'

Without the camping gear, we make light work of the track back to the main road. After ten minutes, a bus stop looms in sight. 'What day is it?'

Becks consults her phone. 'Sunday – God, Joe, I'd completely lost track.'

'We always do, don't we? Mission syndrome. There could be no buses on a Sunday.'

From the back Lenny shouts, 'Truck! Hitch?'

We dive into the bus stop as the artic pulls over. The driver throws open the door. He's the opposite of our Corsican truckie; young, wiry, not on the booze and no sign of a gun. 'Jeez! There's a lot of ya! But yer in luck - ah've got ma big cab today!'

The air brakes go off with a massive hiss, the juggernaut starts moving and our driver throws a sideways glance at Arnaud and Tommaso who are sat in the front with him. 'So – yous are students, are yer?'

Arnaud nods and smiles. 'Yes – we are on holiday, camping. And we have heard that Kyle of Lochalsh is one of the most beautiful parts of Scotland.'

The driver nods. 'You're well right there, laddie.' He hits the mighty horn as a Fiat 500 wanders towards us in the middle of the road. It scuttles back into line.

Becks leans forward. 'Can you hire a boat to go fishing in Kyle of Lochalsh?'

'Sure you can. What sort of fishing? Local or deep sea?

'Deep sea. About ten miles off the coast?'

'What kind've fish are yous looking to catch?'

Lenny comes in quickly. 'Like, sea bass?'

The driver flicks a respectful nod back at Lenny, who is sat behind him. 'If that's your prey, laddie, you're in the right waters. An' I can put you onto a lassie who knows all about fishing sea bass off Kyle of Lochalsh!'

CHAPTER 11

Deep Blue Sea

Seemingly not at all in a hurry to get to his destination, our truckie drives us down to the harbour side and parks. 'It's Shanks Pony from here. Ma name's Dougie, by the way. Dinna bother to gie me yours as I'll ne'er remember six names!'

We walk past a huge pontoon where there's a railway station that's the end of the line from Inverness. The station waiting room also seems to be a railway museum and gift shop and I feel an insane desire to stop and browse. Becks sees me loitering and grabs my hand. 'We'll just have to come back!'

Dougie leads us onwards to a smaller pier where three trawlers are moored, one of them bigger than the others and with a white hull. 'The lassie's called Isla MacDonald,' he confides, 'an' what she doesnae know about fishin' for sea bass isna worth knowing.'

We follow him along the pontoon past heaps of fishing nets and propped up rusty anchors. As we walk, I stare down into the water six feet below and stop dead. 'Catch those jellies!'

'They're just little blobbies, Joe.'

'No Becks, not the little blobbies. Those three huge ones about two feet across – rust coloured with a huge undercarriage!'

Dougie strolls back and nods. 'Those, now, you'd be right to be wary. They grow to eight feet across. Lion's Mane. Their sting can bring on a heart attack, y'know?'

Now all of us are checking out these giant jellies and Lenny takes a photo, before we follow Dougie to the white-hulled trawler, called Sea Eagle. On board, a young woman with short, curly blonde hair in white oilies is draping some nets over the side to dry. She looks up and we see a tanned face and bright blue eyes. Dougie does an exaggerated bow. 'Top of the morning, Miss MacDonald.'

She grins and swings herself over the side of the boat onto the pontoon. 'Dougie, you rogue – you can't be here to pick up a load, as it's a Sunday. And I see you've brought me some company.'

'These guys are interested in doing some deep sea fishing, Isla. Sea bass, in particular. So who else could I possibly recommend?'

The blue eyes look at us appraisingly. 'Are you looking to charter one of my boats?'

Arnaud takes the lead. 'It would be for the day, yes.'

'Have you any experience of handling boats?'

'Not of this type. But I have sailed my father's yacht and also a twelve foot RIB. And I know how to navigate.'

'I have a RIB which might do the job. Come with me.'

Dougie winks. 'I'll be on ma way, then.'

Tommaso offers his hand. 'We are very grateful for the lift – and the introduction!'

With a smile, Dougie shakes. 'Nae problem, laddie!' He goes cheerfully on his way, and we follow Isla along the pontoon to where a tough looking RIB is moored, very like the one we 'borrowed' in Marseille, only about two feet longer.

Isla unties the mooring rope. 'Now, I need to be sure that you know what you're doing.' She nods at Arnaud. 'Jump in and show me how you'd get off this mooring, do some simple, low-speed manoeuvres and then get back onto the mooring. OK?'

'Certainly.'

She hands Arnaud a lifejacket. 'Off you go then!'

Arnaud swings down into the boat and starts the engine. As it roars into life, Isla chucks him the mooring rope and he steers neatly away from the pontoon and out into the harbour. Here, he executes an elegant figure of eight before sliding the RIB with precision back alongside the pontoon.

'Nicely done indeed!' Isla's voice is approving. 'You see, normally I don't hire to under twenty-five year olds. But there's something about you and your friends…'

Becks says quickly, 'That's really very good of you, Miss MacDonald…'

'Oh, call me Isla, please! Now, I'll get you charts

and fishing kit, and while I'm doing that I suggest that you get yourselves a picnic from the bakery up the street.'

There's a stampede to the bakery, where we stock up with baguettes, pasties, sausage rolls, cakes and Coke and treat Becks to everything. On our return, Isla hands out lifejackets, charts, fishing rods and bait, the coastguard number and her mobile number. 'You'd better trust me with your valuables, too, in case someone goes for an unexpected swim.' She takes our wallets and passports off to her office on the quayside while we all get aboard. 'Wait a minute – there's something else you'll be in need of.' She jumps onto Sea Eagle and returns a minute later with binoculars. Michel stows them carefully in the stern.

Holding the mooring line, Isla looks at us thoughtfully and I'm worried that she might be about to change her mind. 'You'll see other fishing boats out there – keep well clear, as you don't want to foul their nets. They won't appreciate that! Oh, and if you see a boat by the name of Black Dog, take yourselves rapidly off in the opposite direction. There's something very odd about a fishing boat that sets off low in the water and returns floating high, like she has no catch aboard.'

The engine roars once more, Isla tosses us the mooring rope and Arnaud swings us out towards the Skye Bridge and the open sea beyond. We pass the lighthouse and look up at the graceful arc of the bridge above us. Looking back, we can still see

Isla's white oilies bright in the sun until the harbour disappears.

—⚓—

'This Black Dog…' Becks mumbles, her mouth full of pasty.

'Goin' out loaded, comin' back empty…' Lenny takes another bite at his tuna baguette.

'A delivery run.' Tommaso takes the tiller so that Arnaud can grab some food.

Michel nods. 'But where?'

I'm starting to feel wonderfully stuffed for the first time in two days. 'How long d'you think it'll take to get to the fourth co-ord?'

'Two hours. Maybe less.' From the way that Tommaso handles the RIB, it's obvious that some of the errands he ran for the Camorra were by boat.

I stare at the rapidly receding coastline and then back at the horizon, where the tiny outline of some kind of craft can be seen. Impossible to get any idea of its size. 'I wish we had radar – then we could check out that boat!'

Tommaso shakes his head. 'Radar cannot always tell you everything, Joe. Try the binoculars.'

Michel passes them over. It takes time to get to know them, but after a few minutes I realise how powerful they are. 'I'm getting the general shape. Looks like a trawler – a bit smaller than Sea Eagle?'

And all the time, we're closing.

'S'pose it's Black Dog?'

'Then we keep out of his way, Becks. But do we follow?'

Tommaso's thought this through already. 'Even if it is Black Dog, if this boat is not heading for the fourth co-ordinate, then we are not interested.'

Arnaud's voice is firm. 'I totally agree with Tommaso. Everyone?'

It's unanimous. And I'm so relieved that the fiery Arnaud gives such respect to Tommaso. I don't think it's just that he loves Tommaso's sister. I think he has an idea of where Tommaso's come from and knows that it was a hell even worse, and more instructive, than his own time in the underworld.

—∿—

We keep closing on the fishing boat, until finally my binoculars get a focus on the writing on her hull. 'She's called Lady of Lochalsh. So no deal.'

Becks takes the binoculars. 'How near are we now to the fourth co-ordinate?'

Tommaso says, 'About three miles. But I do not like the look of the weather.' A sea mist is rolling in from the North West; already the horizon is no longer visible. 'We will have to slow down.'

Everyone strains to keep a lookout as we chug onwards into the cold, damp whiteness. It's eerily quiet, with just the sound of the motor and the small waves slopping up against the hull. We've been moving slowly forward like this for nearly an hour when Michel makes everyone jump. 'Je vois…. quelquechose…'

Tommaso drops the speed to nearly zero. 'We are only a few metres from the fourth co-ordinate.'

Becks calls, 'I can see something huge in the mist!'

That's when Arnaud whispers, 'Dear God!' And we all stare at the fourth co-ordinate, only fifty feet away. I suppose a yachtsman would call it a weird looking catamaran. But to me it looks like a gigantic, supernatural crab, straddling the waters. It must be ninety feet across and another seventy long. All its sides are curved and it's a sea grey/green colour that blends perfectly with the water. At the top is a cabin area with an aerial mast.

Tommaso stares at the monster. 'It is a stealth ship. That is why our radar could not pick it up. Even hovering just above, we could not see it because the camouflage is so good.'

'But it can see us?' Becks voice is nervous.

Lenny calls, 'Boat!'

The dull thrum of a powerful engine is rapidly getting louder. I yell, 'Sounds like it's heading straight for us!' Tommaso guns the engine as a dark shape looms out of the mist, towering above us. As he hurls the RIB out of the way, I catch a glimpse of gold writing on the black hull. 'It's Black Dog!'

The churning wake tosses us around like a toy. Tommaso mutters, 'That was no near-accident. They know exactly what they are doing!'

The engine is screaming as we fly blindly through the water. 'D'you think they'll have another go?'

'I know they will, Joe. They will be enjoying the entertainment.'

Everyone's quiet, keeping a look out as we bump through the waves. Then we hear it – the massive roar of a marine diesel at full power and that huge black hull comes at us again. But this time it's from behind and we have no chance. Tommaso manages to get us out of its direct path, but Black Dog smacks into us with a glancing blow that flips the RIB violently onto one side. Next thing I know, I'm flying through the air and hitting the sea in a belly dive. Gasping with the cold salt water, I listen to the throb of the motor as the boat disappears, leaving a stink of diesel. Something bumps into the back of my head. It's the RIB. Thank God it hasn't capsized. I yell at the top of my voice, 'I've got the RIB! Where is everyone? Shout out your names and I'll keep yelling so you can find me!'

'Lenny and Michel, Joe!' The voices are muffled in the mist.

'Becks! Keep shouting, Joe!'

One by one they appear in the water, bedraggled and cold, with Arnaud and Tommaso arriving last. Tommaso speaks urgently, 'They will be back to mow us down in the water. We will have to dive. Quickly, take off your lifejackets and chuck them in the RIB.'

Feeling the bitter cold seeping into my bones, I struggle out of my lifejacket and help Becks with hers.

'As soon as we hear it, we must dive deep. She will have at least a six foot keel, and we must avoid the prop at all costs. Is everyone ready?'

Teeth chattering, we nod agreement. Then it's a horrible waiting game that seems to take hours; but in reality it's only minutes before that growling engine is heard again.

Tommaso shouts, 'Go!' Taking a huge breath, I kick my way beneath the waves. As soon as I get beneath the surface, the engine noise changes to a thunderous booming. It's like being in a washing machine, churned round and round. I can't see Becks anywhere so I just concentrate on trying to fight my way down. Just as my legs are almost completely numb with cold, a huge dark shadow sweeps over my head; the water around me shakes like an earthquake and the wake from the prop tries to suck me after it. My lungs are screaming now. But Black Dog's ugly bottom has gone. Scrabbling back up to the surface, hoping not to encounter giant jellies, I take great gasps of air and look wildly around for my mates.

From some way off to my left, Lenny shouts, 'Michel and me have the RIB!'

'Keep shouting!'

Once more, the weary swimmers struggle back to our boat. 'Where are Arnaud and Tommaso?'

Becks shakes streaming hair out of her eyes and yells, 'Arnaud! Tommaso!'

Dimly through the fog comes Arnaud's voice, 'I have Tommaso! He is unconscious!'

'Can you manage?'

'Yes! Stay with the RIB and keep shouting!'

We're all listening out in a cold fear that the Dog will come back to bite us again. And now I'm seriously worried about what these water temperatures could be doing to us. We have to get out of the sea soon. Finally, Arnaud appears, swimming on his back with Tommaso in the rescue position. He gasps, 'I think it's the cold! We have to get him into the boat!'

'Right. We'll take a chance on our friends making a return visit. Lenny, can you get in first, and we'll pass Tommaso up to you.'

Lenny pulls himself effortlessly into the RIB and Arnaud, Michel and I lift the unconscious Tommaso towards him.

'You next, Becks. You've got far less body mass than us.'

'Tommaso too.' Her voice wobbles with the cold as Arnaud and I help her into the RIB.

As soon as we're all back on board, Lenny barks an order. 'Recovery position!' With her D of E Bronze, Becks knows about First Aid and she helps Lenny get Tommaso on his side in case he's swallowed water.

Arnaud gets the RIB moving faster than ever before. 'Get your lifejackets on! You will feel the cold less!'

Lenny is taking Tommaso's pulse. 'Got to get him covered!' He looks around the RIB and grabs a set of oilies from beneath the bulwark. Gently, he and Becks ease Tommaso's cold limbs into the thick rubber jacket and trousers and pull the jacket hood over his head. Becks sits on the floor of the RIB with Tommaso's head in her lap to cushion him against the bumps and jolts as we tear through the mist. I stare hard at the whiteness, wondering if I'm imagining it, or is it getting thinner?

Then Michel says, 'Voilà le ciel!'

With the suddenness of its arrival, the mist rolls away in a matter of minutes and the warm sun starts to thaw out our frozen bones. I grab the binoculars, which miraculously have not gone overboard, and anxiously scan the distant waters.

'Well?' Arnaud looks across at me.

'Only the Lady of Lochalsh making her way home.'

'Thank God. And now we must get Tommaso to a hospital.'

'I would prefer not!' Tommaso's eyes are open. He pulls himself into a sitting position, peels the hoodie off his head and turns to Arnaud. 'I owe you my life, my friend. When I felt myself slipping under the waves... I heard your voice.'

'It was lucky I was near you, Tommaso. I could never have forgiven myself...'

Tommaso gazes at the waves. 'We have all been very lucky.'

Becks says softly, 'Why is that, Tommaso?'

'The mist. Normally, Aquila's men would come back and finish off any remaining victims in the water with their guns.'

Isla's waiting on the quayside as we drift up to the mooring. 'Looks like you all took a ducking! And not a sprat in sight?'

'Er, no. The fish didn't have much to worry about with us.' I scramble out and Arnaud chucks me the mooring rope.

Isla looks closely at Tommaso as he comes ashore. 'You're looking rather wan, young man – are you feeling OK?'

He smiles. 'Thank you, I'm fine.'

Becks puts an arm around him. 'What you need is some fish and chips!'

'You're in the right place for that – just up the high street on the right. Now, don't forget your stuff in my office.'

'And I'll settle up with you…'

'Well, you've only been out for half a day, so it'll be half price.'

I've paid Isla and the others are setting off for the fish and chip shop, when a thought strikes me and I go back into her office. 'You know that boat you told us about, Isla.'

'Black Dog?' She frowns, 'You didn't happen to meet with her, did you?'

'Well, we might have done but we couldn't see much in that mist. But I wondered where she's moored?'

Isla's blue eyes look thoughtful. 'Good question. She's not on any of the open moorings. So my guess would be that she's undercover, in one of those pontoon compounds at the far end of the harbour.'

'Right. Thanks, Isla.' I'm heading for the door, when she calls me back.

'Joe… I'm not going to pry as it's none of my business… but the reason why someone has an enclosed mooring is usually because they're not particularly keen on other people seeing what they're loading or unloading.'

'Er… yeah.'

'So if I were you, I'd keep away. They may not be the friendliest types.'

—⁓—

We take our fish and chips down to the harbour side and sit munching them on benches, our sodden clothes soon drying in the warm sun. On the benches to our right, a coach party of pensioners are contentedly doing the same; their driver is sitting in the coach, eating an ice cream and reading The Mirror.

'That a spare vinegar, Lenny?'

He chucks the sachet over. So far on this mission, I'm amazed at how much we've had to eat. My main memory of our other adventures, apart from the fear, is the gnawing hunger. Once everyone has chucked their rubbish in the bin, I go and sit next to Tommaso. 'How are you feeling, Bro?'

A slow smile. 'Not quite brother, Joe.'

'Near enough for me. Mind you, you haven't

met my little brother Jack yet. Not sure you'd like him. He keeps fish and plays the saxophone.' Tommaso laughs and it's good to see him relax a bit. 'Right, I'm taking orders for ice creams. Did you see what they had in that chippy?'

—⁓—

When everyone's completely stuffed, I quietly tell them what Isla told me about the likely mooring place of Black Dog. And about how we might like to take a look. Lenny nods. 'S'do it!'

'OK, but we don't want to attract attention. So let's split into three groups. We can communicate by phone 'cause teenagers are always on their phones, so it'll look normal.'

We end up with Arnaud and Tommaso in front, followed at a distance by me and Becks, and Michel and Lenny bringing up the rear. After a few minutes, Arnaud calls. 'Do you know which pontoon compound? We're next to the first one.'

'No. How many are there?'

'Six. But three are open and so probably empty.'

'And the one you're at?'

'Is closed. But Tommaso says the lock is easy if Becks has a hair grip?'

'Do you do hairgrips, Becks?'

She rummages in her handbag. Locating the break-in tool, she catches up with Arnaud and Tommaso and surreptitiously hands it over. From the outside, the compound looks like a small

150

aircraft hangar, with a wide vertical sliding door and a padlocked handle in the middle.

Tommaso goes to work with the hair grip while the rest of us keep watch. Along the quayside, the pensioners are boarding their coach. Tommaso and Arnaud lift the door slightly and peer underneath it. Then they close it again and Tommaso replaces the padlock. Arnaud calls, 'There is a catamaran moored inside which certainly is not Black Dog.'

'OK, try the next.'

He calls back. 'It is full of antique furniture and no boat.'

'Third time lucky?'

At the third compound, after Tommaso has picked the padlock and looked inside, Arnaud flicks a quick nod at me before the pair of them lift the door further and slip into the compound. Arnaud calls. 'We will need lookouts, on the harbour side and outside the door.' I call Michel and Lenny and they casually start to take up stations, while Becks and I take cautious glances around before following Arnaud and Tommaso. Inside, the mooring is unoccupied. Parked next to it is a black Range Rover with heavily tinted glass. Next to the Range Rover are two wooden crates.

With his knife, Tommaso prises a slat off one of the crate lids. I've never seen anything as evil looking as the rifles lying inside; the dark grey barrels with their dull sheen are unusually long and slim. Arnaud whispers, 'High velocity – like the one that nearly killed my father.'

Tommaso taps the slat back down and turns his attention to the Range Rover. He finds the driver's door open and the key in the ignition. 'Joe, help me get the sat nav working. We need to find out where these guns are coming from.' We get in and after a few minutes of playing around with the sat nav, we find the driver's favourites. 'Becks, can you enter this on your phone. It looks like a private address.' He reels off a set of co-ordinates.

Suddenly, Lenny calls through. 'Black Dog!'

'Quick!' As we slide out of the compound, I say to Lenny, 'We need to split up again. You and Michel head for the Sea Eagle pontoon.' Arnaud and Tommaso make for the town centre, while Becks and I try to stroll nonchalantly towards the coach, which is standing with its engine running. I flick a quick glance out to sea and my heart thumps as I see that dark hull powering into the harbour, churning up a large bow wave.

—◉—

We all meet up again in the Co-op cafe, and over Coke and cakes we take a look at the route to wherever those guns are coming from. Becks frowns, zooming in on her sat nav. 'It's quite a hike… goes right past the road to the campsite.'

'In that case, let's collect the radios. If we get into the hills there'll be no phone signal.'

Arnaud nods, 'Good idea, Joe. And the torches.'

Tommaso looks at me. 'Are you alright, Joe?'

'I just wish I knew if tonight is going to take me closer to Dad or not.'

'You are thinking he might be a prisoner on the stealth ship?'

'Yeah…'

CHAPTER 12

Line of Fire

Amazingly, we find out that there is a bus that will take us as far as the campsite, so we're back at the tents within an hour. Armed with radios and torches we set off for Destination X, as Becks calls it. Everyone trudges quietly at first and every time we hear a powerful engine we look round, in case it's the black Range Rover. Tommaso has memorised the reg number: BL13 DOG. Becks comments, 'How sad is that?'

After an hour of brisk walking, it's getting dark and drops of rain are falling. Becks studies her phone. 'Three miles to go.'

That's when I start to get the shakes. With every step I take, I see Dad's carefree smile and blue eyes. Then I get a vision of something awful happening to him. I'm really starting to go to pieces when an arm goes round my shoulders. Tommaso whispers, 'We are here for you, Joe, just as much as we know you are here for us.'

I find myself murmuring, 'All for one and one for all.' And suddenly, the phantoms blow away and disappear into the rainy night.

Shortly after Becks announces, 'One mile', the stone wall begins. Running along the road on our left behind a ditch and towering above us in the gathering dark, it's around twelve feet high and made out of layered granite stones. Tendrils of ivy grow upwards, embracing the dark stones with their spiky leaves.

Arnaud shines his torch. 'It looks like it could be the boundary of a large estate.'

'Where Aquila's playing Lord of the Manor?'

Lenny shouts, 'Range Rover!' We flatten ourselves in the ditch. Xenon headlights approach rapidly with the roar of a V8 and the 4x4 blasts past us.

'Yuk!' Becks brushes mud off her jeans.

'Did you see the reg?'

Lenny shakes his head. 'But it was black.'

All the way through the next mile the wall is with us. It's completely unbroken and solid except at one point, where my torch picks out a green wooden door about ten feet tall and five feet wide, half covered with trailing ivy. Making a mental note, I hurry to catch up with the others. We walk on for another twenty minutes and then stop. The wall has turned into a pair of tall black cast-iron gates. Beyond, a gravel drive snakes into woodlands. The gates are open.

Tommaso waves at us to back off. 'Sure to be cameras.'

I whisper, 'I might have found somewhere…?'

We jog back to the green door. Tommaso shines his torch everywhere, probes the ivy and tests the latch. He shakes his head. 'It is too easy to lift. It should be rusty and seized. They have set this up for intruders.'

Becks runs a hand through a frizzy red curl. 'So… what do we do? Climb the wall?'

'Yes. But far away from the gates.'

—⁀∞⁀—

I catch Becks as she lets go and drops. Lenny and Michel swing down effortlessly. Arnaud and Tommaso get over just before a truck with blazing headlamps roars past. We stand completely still, looking around us. We're in deep woods which are silent, apart from a slight rustling of leaves. Very faintly through the trees glows a pale light. Tommaso whispers, 'There could be concealed cameras in these trees. We must try not to use the torches.' We pause for a little longer to get our eyes accustomed to the dark and then start to move slowly towards the distant light.

As our feet swish through the knee high grass, the moon sails out from behind the clouds and something metallic flashes high up in a tree. I stop dead to stare at it, and see Tommaso doing the same. We exchange looks and he nods. The others have now stopped and are looking at the camera. There's no way of telling if it's actually working. Wordlessly, we skirt round the tree with the eye and continue towards the light.

As we get closer, more lights appear. Reaching the edge of the trees, we pause to survey what lies ahead. The first light is attached to the outside of a long, stone-built barn, its large bulk shadowy in the moonlight. Another barn stands at a right-angle to this one. The gravel drive that led from the main entrance runs past the barns, and on up to a huge mansion. A flight of steps leads up to the massive entrance door beneath a stone porch with Greek columns. Parked by the steps is a black Range Rover. I whisper to Michel, 'Can you see the reg plate?'

'DOG.'

My heart is thumping as we creep round the long barn, trying to see what's inside. We find a wooden stable door, and Tommaso tests the latch. To our surprise, it lifts with a squeak and the door swings open. Lenny whispers, 'Michel 'n me will keep a look out'. We share out the radios, one each for Lenny and Michel and one that Tommaso takes for us four intruders. As Lenny and Michel take up position outside, we slip inside the barn.

It's completely dark and there's a weird smell that I can't quite work out. 'I'll have to use the torch.' The beam picks out windows that are boarded up, some that aren't and a stone floor. It glints on three rifles similar to the ones we saw in the crate, lying on a trestle table.

Then Becks hisses, 'Look! There by the window!'

'Get down!' Arnaud pushes Becks and me to the

floor. Right at the end of the barn are the silhouettes of the heads and shoulders of three men. I stare, waiting for them to shoot at us but not one of them moves a muscle.

Tommaso whispers, 'They are dummies – targets. We are in a shooting range.' And now I remember what that smell is. Cordite; what you get after a gun is fired.

As the four of us re-join Lenny and Michel outside, headlights split the darkness, there's the purr of a powerful engine and a silver Aston Martin DB11 glides up the drive, stopping outside the house. A tall, white-haired man in a dinner jacket and a younger man also in a smart black suit get out and go up the steps.

'D'you know those dudes, Tommaso?'

He shakes his head, 'Not by sight, no.'

'OK, let's have a go at getting into the other barn.'

This door is less co-operative, but it yields in a few minutes to Becks' hairgrip and Tommaso's clever fingers. He looks cautiously inside. 'There is an alarm system,' he nods at the switch panel, 'but it is not set.'

I stare at the unblinking green light on the panel. 'Seems like they're not too worried about intruders, then.'

'I suspect that the CCTV system in the grounds does most of the work for them.'

Arnaud whispers impatiently, 'So let's get inside shall we?'

Lenny and Michel take up stations again at either end of the barn and we move warily into the blackness within, Tommaso and I bringing up the rear behind Becks and Arnaud. He flicks on his torch and we stare at the production lines of guns in various stages of assembly. There's one for machine guns, another for handguns and a third with those vicious looking rifles that we saw in Kyle of Lochalsh. The sight of so many killing machines chills me to the bone. Arnaud breathes, 'No more room for any doubt then, about who this place belongs to.'

Tommaso takes three quick photos with his phone.

Lenny radios through, 'Nother car jus' turned up.'

I take a deep breath. 'Time to check out the house.'

We all gather outside the barn door as Tommaso pulls it to. 'We may need to take cover here, so I am leaving it unlocked.'

'What was the car, Lenny?'

'Small Fiat wasn't it Michel? Maybe staff?'

Michel nods. 'Je crois.'

Between the arms factory and the house is an expansive lawn, but at least it's dotted with fancily cut bushes for cover, and clouds are now covering the moon. We make it to the house and take a line along the side of the building, keeping to the shadows and looking out for cameras. Around the back of the building is a far humbler door than the one at the front. There's a light on inside; through the window, it looks like a large kitchen. No sign of anyone. The door is open. Lenny and Michel go on lookout and the remaining four of us slip inside.

It's what you might expect of a kitchen in a stately home. There's two of everything. Two cookers, one an Aga and the other electric. A wooden sink with rows of sparkling crystal glassware on the draining board. And a porcelain sink with a load of oven dishes waiting for attention. Becks mutters, 'Don't they know about dishwashers?'

I whisper, 'There's two over there... now we've got to move fast if people are turning up. Becks and Tommaso, do you feel like tackling the upper floors?'

Arnaud whispers, 'There is only one radio left.'

Tommaso shrugs. 'If we are caught, it will be of little use. So you and Joe keep the radio, my friend.' Becks nods. With Tommaso in the lead, they carefully slide through the door at the far end of the kitchen.

'Arnaud, we need to listen in on these people – they could let slip where Dad is being held.'

He nods. 'So we find out where they are gathered.'

Seconds after we leave the kitchen, there's the sound of an argument and footsteps approaching; we dodge through a door into what turns out to be a cupboard full of brooms and vacuum cleaners.

'It's nae fair, Mister Campbell, this is the eighth night in a row I've had to do overtime. Ah missed ma Gran's birthday last Sunday for him!'

'He's not a man you should argue with, y'know that, Lizzie.'

Their voices fade as they go into the kitchen and we exit the cupboard. Slipping along dimly lit corridors, we strain to listen for a footfall but meet no one. Then we turn into a corridor that is wider and more brightly lit. 'I think we must be getting close to the main entrance.'

Arnaud nods. We peer cautiously round the wall and see a grand hallway, with a fancy gold ceiling and a huge candelabra. A door off the hall on the left is open and there's the sound of conversation. But it's all so exposed and brightly lit that we hesitate. Then voices from behind drive us rapidly through the first available door, which happens to be next to the one that's open.

It takes a few seconds to get used to the darkness and see the wooden staircase that spirals upwards. Arnaud whispers, 'This could lead to some kind of gallery.' Gingerly, we creep up the stairs. At the top, an archway opens out onto a narrow balcony with a balustrade made from ornate woodwork. Perfect for spying through the small holes and not being seen. We edge up to it on all fours and look down at Aquila's little party.

He's sprawled over a Chesterfield sofa, still wearing the boots with the spurs. The long Mac is tossed over a chair with the Stetson on top of it. I can't see a gun but I can't imagine him without one. A glass full of whisky is in his hand and he's waving it around, boasting about something. The two dudes from the Aston Martin, one white-haired and the other with dark hair, are sat in chairs opposite. To my surprise, the older man looks less than impressed by what his host is saying, while the younger man looks positively bored.

'So there you have it,' Stetson takes a swig from his glass. 'Your investments are completely safe with me, gentlemen. You could call them bullet-proof, if you'll excuse the pun.'

Arnaud and I exchange looks. So this is about money. Are these gentlemen getting a bit uneasy about their dosh in Aquila's hands? The white haired guy leans forward. 'We have news of an ex-SAS agent who for some time has been hell-bent on, shall we say, bringing your operations to book? What are you doing about him?'

'He is being dealt with. He presents no more threat.'

The young guy swigs mineral water from a bottle. He frowns. 'So where is Commander Julius Grayling right now, exactly?'

Aquila's eyes look more hooded and his free hand twitches slightly. 'As I said, he can do no more harm.'

The younger man puts the bottle of mineral water down. 'And as *I* said, where exactly are you holding him?'

'NTK, old chap.'

The younger dude's voice is as cold as iced tea. 'We *do* need to know, *old chap*. Otherwise our investment sprouts legs and walks.'

Arnaud's face is a picture of astonishment and mine must look the same. This guy isn't afraid of Aquila. Who on earth is he? I take a closer look. Short, dark hair, an expensive tan, fashionably unshaven and with brown eyes, he could be Italian or maybe Corsican. And could he be the older man's son? There is some family resemblance in the broad forehead.

Aquila's spur rips into the Chesterfield's leather as he swings off the sofa and lights a fat cigar. 'On the ship, of course. Where else? It's completely invisible.'

The younger dude takes another sip of mineral water. 'It had better be.'

And we have it, that precious information. Arnaud and I are inching backwards towards the stairs when there's a brisk knock at the door and two helmeted security guards walk in with Becks and Tommaso. Becks is pale but very calm. Tommaso's thin face gives nothing away. Aquila smiles. He would, wouldn't he? This has got him off the hook. He's preening himself as he swaggers over to Becks. 'How touching, pretty one. You just couldn't keep away, could you?'

Becks' green eyes are glittering. Her voice is casual. 'You do seem to have a fatal attraction.'

More preening. 'How charming of you...'

'And anyway, I'm bored with being on the side of the great and the good.'

Aquila's eyes fix on Becks with an interest that makes me go cold all over. 'Is what I'm hearing a proposition? What kind of .. .services… could you possibly offer me?'

'Simple. I know a great deal about Commander Julius Grayling's network.' Becks shakes her guard's hand off her arm and sits down, smoothing her hair. 'I know names and contact numbers and how they operate. You know you'll never get that out of Julius Grayling, no matter how much you torture him.'

Stetson takes a drag on the cigar. 'Very interesting. But you don't quite look the traitor type…'

Becks stands and her eyes are green fire. 'Then take another look! I've had it with being treated like a pathetic teenage girl without a clever idea in her head. Always just tagging along instead of being the mover and shaker. Those days are over. And if you don't want my information, I know others who will! Which way do you want it?"

The guests seem mesmerised by Becks' performance. Aquila can't stop looking at her; it makes my skin crawl. 'Well, well. Not just beauty but brains as well.' He turns to Tommaso. 'And what have you to offer me, you ingrate? Tired of life in Napoli?'

Tommaso says quietly, 'I've got a better aim even than you. Want to take me on?'

Aquila stares at this skinny, tired-looking boy. 'You know, I could have you shot like a dog for just saying that?'

Unblinkingly, Tommaso returns the stare. 'But then you'd never find out, would you?'

The dark haired man is looking interested.

'What's the matter, old chap? Afraid of losing to a child?' He couldn't have put it better.

Stetson barks at the guards, 'Set up the indoor range!' He turns to his guests. 'No doubt you wish to be present?'

The white haired man nods. 'We wouldn't miss it for anything.'

Stetson turns to Becks. 'And you, my dear, are coming too.'

She shrugs. 'I know how good he is. But I'll come along.'

Arnaud and I wait until the room is empty then radio to Lenny and Michel. 'They've got Becks and Tommaso. He's challenged Aquila to a shooting contest. Can you go on the watch outside the firing range?' Then Arnaud and I cautiously take the back door route out of the house and slip through the shadows towards the long barn. 'I've seen Becks do Hollywood big time, but that takes the Oscar.'

Arnaud shakes his head. 'Putting herself in harm's way like that, it's a huge risk.'

'And Tommaso is doing the same.'

—✺—

By the time we get down to the long barn, Michel and Lenny are in position outside at the far end. I gesture to ask if Aquila's party has gone in and Lenny gives the thumbs up. They've found a window that isn't boarded up and we find one at the other end near the door. Our window has a bullet hole in it, so we can hear as well.

Inside, the barn is brightly lit by overhead strip lights. Aquila's two black-suited guests are standing in quiet conversation near the door. Her face expressionless, Becks stands close to Tommaso, next to the trestle table where the three rifles are lying. Under Aquila's instructions, the two guards move six dummies into position, hanging on wires from the ceiling at the far end. They're hardboard cut-outs of the top half of a human, with a circle and sight lines in the centre of the chest and another circle with no sight lines in the centre of the forehead. The targets are so far away, I can barely see the bulls-eyes.

Aquila unlocks a large safe in the corner and takes out a handgun which he holds out to Tommaso. Tommaso shakes his head. 'This type is always jamming.'

Aquila's hook-nosed face is a combination of annoyance and grudging respect. Muttering, 'Beggars can't be choosers, brat,' he reaches into the safe again and takes out a different gun.

Tommaso nods. 'Glock is good.'

'I'm *so* glad you think so. Right, the rules are simple. Three dummies each. Three shots to the heart and three to the head. Capisce?'

'Capisco.'

'And being the challenged party, I have the right to go first.'

The younger guest steps forward. 'And we'll be the judges. When you're ready, then?'

Aquila whips up his gun and fires six shots really fast into each of his three dummies.

Arnaud whispers, 'Showy, but is it accurate?'

It's impossible to see from where we are. The guards are moving towards Aquila's dummies when the younger judge calls out, 'No! Leave them until all shots are fired.'

And then it's Tommaso's turn. Calmly, he raises his gun. After each shot he takes aim again, with a rhythm so quick and precise it's like percussion. Arnaud and I exchange looks. 'He is a crack shot, as good as your father and mine, Joe.'

'I guess in the Camorra, he had to be to protect himself.'

The guards bring the dummies for inspection. The younger judge frowns. 'Just one clean hole for the heart and the head on all dummies from your brat, old chap. Whereas your efforts...' he shakes his head, 'don't you think you should hire this young man on rather good terms?'

Aquila's voice is ever so slightly slurred. 'That was child's play. Now, we do moving targets. Live meat.' He switches on the split-screen monitor on the trestle table; and there we are, Arnaud and me, Lenny and Michel, all on camera, frozen like rabbits in front of headlights.

Lenny radios, 'S'go!'

'We can't till we know what the game is!'

The guests look on, interested at this turn of events. Aquila rests the barrel of his handgun casually at Tommaso's throat. 'If you're serious about joining me, brat, then you won't hesitate to make dead meat of your former colleagues. You have ten minutes to take them out. If not, then I will have no choice but to make dead meat of the pair of you.' He reaches for one of the rifles on the trestle table and throws it at Tommaso. 'Happy hunting!' Tommaso catches it, never taking his eyes off Aquila.

Becks says casually, 'Give me a gun and I'll give him a hand.'

The pale eyes look Becks slowly up and down and I want to blast Aquila into the next world. 'Oh, that wouldn't do at all, my dear. You're the live bait. You stay here with me.'

—ᴍ—

As Tommaso heads for the barn door, the four of us run like hell into the trees. We can hear him firing shots as he follows. Arnaud calls, 'I think he's taking out the cameras!'

We slow down and Tommaso joins us. In those three minutes, my brain's been going so fast it hurts. 'We've got seven minutes left. Arnaud, can you check out the cars up by the house – try and find one with a driver who's been careless with his keys.' Arnaud sprints off into the woods. 'Tommaso, how are we going to get Becks out?'

He turns the rifle over in his hands. 'I think I can disarm Aquila – he looks very drunk.'

'What about the guards?'

'They were following me until I started shooting out the cameras.'

'So they could've gone back to the barn?'

'Empty handed? They wouldn't dare. They are probably securing the gates.'

'D'you think our friends in suits are armed?'

'There's no way of knowing.'

'OK, let's go.' With Lenny and Michel bringing up the rear to keep an eye out for the guards, Tommaso and I sprint back to the barn. I glance at my watch. 'Two minutes.'

Tommaso looks cautiously through the window. 'He's still holding the handgun and saying something to Becks. There's no sign of the suits or the guards.'

'God, we don't want him alone with Becks!'

'Ready? Go!' He kicks the door open. Aquila starts to take aim but Tommaso shoots first and the gun flies out of Aquila's hand, blowing a hole in the wall. Before he can move, Lenny and Michel wrench his arms behind his back. 'You little bastards!' He struggles furiously until Lenny knocks him out with a karate chop to the back of the neck. He slumps to the floor and Becks ties him tight with the wire from one of the dummies. She's obviously enjoying wrenching the wire really tight, and I wonder what the perv was saying to her.

Seeing Aquila starting to stir, I grab another length of wire. 'We need to lash him to the table.'

Becks gets to work. 'Happy to oblige!'

Michel peers warily out of the barn door. 'Car.'

'Let's hope it's Arnaud.'

Seconds later, headlights blaze through the

woods and the black Range Rover roars up to us with Arnaud at the wheel. The five of us pile in and he stamps on the accelerator. 'Was the Aston still there, Arnaud?'

He shakes his head, flinging the steering wheel from side to side to dodge trees. So now both the guards and the suits are on my mind. 'I think we could have a problem at the gate.'

We bump through the trees then hit the gravel drive. Arnaud slows as the headlamps reveal a gate that is now closed. At the same moment there's a Smack and a star shape appears in the windscreen. 'Get down!' On full power, Arnaud wrenches the wheel round and we take off in the opposite direction; but not before the rear screen collects its own spider's web. Cautiously, we raise our heads as the Range Rover roars back up the drive towards the house. Arnaud looks at me, 'There's got to be another way out of this place!'

'There's that green wooden door… but I'm not sure if it's wide enough. And it's horribly close to the gate.'

'We have no choice but to try!' Arnaud swings the Range Rover back into the trees, weaving between them at breakneck speed and giving the two barns a wide berth. The wall looms ahead. Impatiently, Arnaud asks, 'Right or left?'

Becks says, 'I'm sure it's right.'

Seconds later, we get to the door in the wall. Lenny jumps out to open it. 'S'locked. Michel!' Michel joins him and they link arms to charge at the door. Three goes and the door starts to give. And all the time I'm sure I can see approaching torchlight. A fourth charge and Crump! The door disintegrates.

Lenny and Michel jump back into the Range Rover. Arnaud has folded the door mirrors flat. Now, he rams the accelerator to the floor and we charge at this space that everyone knows is too narrow. There's a graunching crunch as we make contact with the wooden posts and both door mirrors fly off into the night. But we're through and just in time, as another bullet whacks into the tailgate. The road is empty as we set off for Kyle of Lochalsh and the stealth ship.

Lenny clips on his seatbelt. 'Shame 'bout the mirrors.'

Sitting in the back seat next to Becks, I can't work something out. 'What happened to the suits, Becks?'

She pulls her hair up into a ponytail. 'Immediately after Tommaso left, the younger one took a call on his mobile. Then he exchanged a few words with the white-haired guy which I couldn't hear. They left in a hurry, saying something to Aquila in Italian. Sounded quite rude, like a b★★★★★★ word, questioning parentage?'

Tommaso says quietly. 'I think things are not looking so good for our friend with the hat.'

'How's that, Tommaso?'

'The suits were not at all pleased about your father getting so close to bringing Aquila down. It sounds like, after his general display of incompetence this evening, they are taking their money elsewhere. What you heard Becks, was 'basta' – meaning 'enough'.'

Arnaud accelerates to 80. 'If that is true, your father is now in even greater danger, Joe. Aquila will be seeking revenge.'

CHAPTER 13

Invisible

Dawn is starting to tip the Skye Bridge with a pale pink light as we pull up next to Isla MacDonald's pontoon. The RIB is moored in the same place as before. We jump down into the boat and Arnaud starts the engine. Casting off, I notice that Tommaso has brought his rifle. He sees me looking at it. 'The bullet that took Aquila's gun away from him was the last. But it will be useful as a deterrent.'

'Nice one.'

The RIB's engine screams as Arnaud forces every last bit of power out of it and we bump and crash across the choppy waves. The brightening dawn tints the waves on the horizon a deepening rose colour. We all keep watch, dreading the sight of Black Dog's ugly bulk hurtling towards us.

Becks says, 'I suppose they could already be on the water and after us…'

Tommaso nods. 'We have bought ourselves very little time.'

I stare at the horizon. 'D'you think they're faster than us?'

'That marine diesel is very powerful. But Black Dog is a heavy boat.'

The breeze is stiffening and from time to time, water splashes over the bows, chilling us to the bone. I wonder what's happening to Dad. I haven't heard his voice in a while. Does that mean he's nearer, or further away?

—⁓—

Half an hour later Michel is scanning the horizon ahead of us. He has the binoculars fixed on a specific point. 'There is something...' He passes the binoculars to Lenny.

'Michel's right. 'Bout two miles.'

Staring in that direction, all I can see is something slightly odd about where the sky meets the sea. It's like a blurring of the waves and the clouds, so you can't make out one from the other. Like a mirage.

As we get closer, the mirage turns into a ghost-like shape coming at us out of the water. The ghost gets more and more enormous until it's towering above us. And the stealth ship is suddenly and starkly there. Hunched and aggressive, its massive crab shape sends a shiver through me. Arnaud slows the engine and we drift towards the five blue-grey hulls that make up the water legs of the stealth ship. As we approach, I become aware of a dull humming that seems to come from deep inside the ship. It's such a low frequency that I wonder if it's my ears. I touch Michel's arm. 'Can you hear it?'

He nods. 'Not a diesel.'

Tommaso whispers, 'It is probably nuclear powered. In Aquila's business they would need to cover vast distances without having to visit a port.'

Now I feel really cold. 'Nuclear? With all that ammo on board?'

He shrugs. 'Just another risk that you take in the illegal arms business…'

Arnaud steers us to the right of the centre hull and suddenly we're in the shades. It's weird, sliding beneath this monster. Like it could suddenly squat down and push us beneath the waves forever. Arnaud's voice is impatient. 'Any ideas on how we're going to get in?'

Michel points to a round, hinged plate at the top of the centre hull. It's around twenty feet above us; a metal ladder welded to the hull leads up to it. In the middle of the plate is an iron handle.

Arnaud nods at Michel. 'You're our ace climber. You go first.'

Arnaud manoeuvres the RIB up to the steps and I lash it to the ladder. Tommaso whispers, 'Test the handle to see if it will open. Look out for sensors!' Michel jumps lightly onto the ladder. The wind is starting a full scale blow now and the hulls are moving, water slapping and spray foaming around them. We're getting thrown around in the RIB. But Michel makes the plate with no apparent effort. He reaches out for the handle. It turns easily in his hand. I guess they're not expecting visitors in a ship that no one can see.

I give Michel the thumbs up and he turns the handle 180 degrees. The plate swings open. Beyond is a dimly lit tunnel about four feet in diameter. Michel climbs in and braces himself with his feet against the tunnel sides. 'You go next, Becks.' Arnaud and I steady her in the tossing RIB as she reaches for the ladder.

'Whooh!' Her foot slips on the first rung but she pulls herself back, hanging on tight as the huge hulls move restlessly in the waves. Michel holds out a hand to her and she crawls in past him. The rest of us follow on up until we're all sitting in the tunnel, Tommaso with the gun over his knees. Michel reaches down and closes the hatch.

Becks whispers to me, 'Is this some kind of airlock?'

'Yeah. And it wasn't designed to take six people. Tommaso, you need to lead, now.' He climbs on, round a corner in the tunnel. We follow, breathing air that feels increasingly thin and stuffy. Then suddenly, clean air wafts down to us and Tommaso calls, 'I think your father could have escaped, Joe!'

We climb out of the airlock into a control room. A semi-circular window looks out onto the sea, with banks of twinkling and beeping instruments beneath it. There are three gyroscopic seats fixed to the floor next to the dials. As the stiffening wind makes the stealth ship move with the waves, the seats adjust to compensate, staying level. Strapped into two of the seats, expertly bound and gagged, are two uniformed guards who glare at us in an angry silence.

Four doors lead off the cabin. Becks and Arnaud take one, Lenny and Michel another. Tommaso and I cautiously open the third. It's like a huge, walk-in cupboard; on the floor lie heavy duty metal cases five feet high. Tommaso prises the top one open with his knife. The lid is heavy; it takes a massive heave for us to open it. In the dark interior of the case is a large, round metal body with spines that gleam dully. 'I've never seen a mine like, face to face.'

Tommaso helps me to close the lid. 'Nor do you want to again.'

Back in the cabin, the others have had similar life-enhancing experiences with high velocity rifles, machine guns, grenades and rocket launchers. There remains the fourth door. Inside is a small, windowless cabin with a bunk bed. The walls are bare. There's an indentation in the bed where someone could have been sitting. On the floor is a single handcuff and chain. The chain has been burned through.

At the same moment as we're taking this in, Lenny calls from the window, 'Black Dog!' The Dog is at anchor while Aquila and the two guards from the house motor towards us in a RIB. I look at the hatch to the airlock. 'Can we block it to keep them out? What about using some of those munitions crates?'

Tommaso shakes his head. 'There is a risk that

he would shoot through the hatch.' He looks at the instrument banks. 'If we had longer, I could probably work out how to get this ship moving, but…'

'Has it got anything like, missiles that we could scare them off with?'

'Stealth ships are rarely armed – they rely on their invisibility.'

'That's not much help now…'

Tommaso looks at his rifle. 'He knows that one wrong shot could send the nuclear reactor into meltdown. He does not know that this gun has no ammo.'

My brain wakes up. 'And if someone else has the rifle, it could work even better. He knows how well you shoot… but…'

'Okay dudes, give it to me. Everyone knows girls can't shoot. Especially the perv.' Becks takes the rifle from Tommaso. In silence, we wait for them to arrive.

The two guards are the first through the airlock. Becks levels the rifle at them and they freeze. Aquila climbs into the cabin and she turns the gun towards him. 'Don't move.'

The hooded eyes glitter. 'And what if I do?'

'I'll shoot you.'

Whipping his hand from his pocket, he points a small pistol at her head. 'Not if I shoot you first, dear heart. Now, be a good girl and hand it over.'

She hesitates and my heart stops. 'Do it, Becks, for God's sake!' She chucks the rifle at his feet.

'Well, well, bad pennies do have a habit, don't they?' Aquila glances into the empty bunk room while his men untie the nervous-looking guards. 'You will be suitably disciplined for allowing this to happen.'

He turns to us. 'Fortunately, with your arrival, it will not be at all difficult to incentivise Commander Grayling to return. Get in the boat.'

None of us moves a muscle. 'Oh, we're playing silly buggers, are we?' He waves on the guards. 'Get them into the RIB!'

The guards hesitate. I guess they're working out who to grab first. In that split-second, Lenny moves like lightning and lands a punch that would fell an ox on the guard nearest him; the guard goes down. At the same time, Michel leaps on the guard opposite him, brings him to the ground like a lion on a deer and bangs his head hard on the floor; out for the count. Tommaso's guard makes a run for him and effortlessly Tommaso uses the momentum to tip the guy over his back and smash him against the wall, knocking him out. Arnaud, in the meantime, is karate kicking his guard into oblivion.

And I'm watching Aquila, who has his arm round Becks' throat and the pistol pressed against her right ear. I never take my eyes from hers. She never looks away from me.

Breathing heavily, the guys realise what's happened and stare in horror at the gun. Aquila is smiling as he releases the safety catch. 'Jolly good show. Those idiots needed a thrashing. Now, as I'm getting rather tired of repeating myself…?'

As we get into Aquila's RIB, I notice with a shock that Isla's RIB is no longer there. Has Dad taken it? Is he closer than we thought? Then our boat wallops into a wave, chucking us around, and I feel a new fear. 'You don't have to keep holding that thing at her head! We're hardly going to jump you...'

'As long as I'm holding this thing at her head, safety catch off, no you're not going to do anything, sonny.'

Black Dog's dark hull looms over us and I scan the boat for any signs of life. There's no one on deck and no faces at the portholes. 'Pull alongside and be quick about it!' Lenny leans out and grabs one of the fenders, pulling the RIB towards a ladder attached to the side of the boat. 'Now you all go up the ladder. And no playing around unless you want a bullet in your back.' Stetson follows last with Becks. 'Down into the cabin – move it!'

As we climb down the steep steps into the cabin, the diesel roars into life. So Aquila has at least one crew member on board. He pushes Becks towards a chair that's fixed to the floor, one of six around a rectangular table.

Aquila points his gun at Tommaso. 'Tie them up, brat. And I'll be watching you.' He chucks some coils of rope at Tommaso. Tommaso is conspicuously careful tying up Michel, Lenny, Arnaud and Becks. When he gets to me, he surreptitiously twists a loop of rope round my hand to give me some slack before lashing my shoulders tightly. Aquila drags Tommaso to a chair and ties his hands and his feet. He surveys us all with satisfaction. 'I'm going to make you sorry you were ever born, dear hearts.' He looks at Becks. 'And I have some very special plans for you, pretty one.' I catch a glimpse of Tommaso's blue eyes, blazing with hatred. The engine revs up and the boat swings round, heading for the distant shore.

For the first five minutes or so, Aquila plays with the handgun, loading a fresh cartridge. Then he gets up and goes to a wall-mounted cupboard, takes out a bottle of whisky and pours himself a large slug. He's put the handgun inside the cupboard. As soon as his back's turned, I start to work at the rope. Outside, the wind is strengthening and the sky is darkening with ragged black clouds. Black Dog rolls and wallows in the troughs of the waves.

Steadying himself against the motion of the boat, Aquila turns back towards us. Instantly, my hands are still. His voice has that slight slur in it again. 'He's your father, isn't he, this eminent Commander Grayling?'

I don't answer.

'Thought you'd follow your old man into the same line of business, did you?'

Silence. I wait for the blow to the head. But this time, it doesn't come. He takes another swallow of whisky. 'Very foolish, when you're no better at it than he is.'

Still, no one replies. I stare out of the windows; the waves are getting bigger. As the boat plunges into the bottom of a swell, a torrent of water pours onto the deck and down the ladder into the cabin. The wind is howling now, with gusts buffeting the cabin. Momentarily diverted by the weather, our host looks out at the storm-ridden sky; I work my rope looser, and keep working as he pours himself another whisky. Now my rope is good to go. I can see the gun still in the cupboard. The only issue is, has he got another gun in his pockets?

Suddenly, the engine stops, like it's just been turned off. We're drifting, tossed sideways from one wave to the next. 'What the… ?' Aquila is nearly toppled by the violent motion of the boat. Staggering slightly, he makes for the steps. As his feet disappear, I drop the ropes, jump from my seat and lunge for the handgun.

Becks is looking up the steps. She shakes her head. 'No….!'

At the same time as I hear the shot I feel a blow to my lower leg like a machete and I'm thrown on my back. The last thing I hear before a red curtain comes down is Becks' cry and another shot. Time stretches out into a void after that. Dimly, with the horror that the second bullet was for Becks and this pain to end all pains, I see two figures locked in combat on deck. As the boat plunges, waves crashing over the prow, they're flung from side to side. Then I can't bear it anymore and dark takes me.

—⁓—

In the dream, this giant tooth keeps gnawing away at my leg. I'm falling down an endless hole, being tossed around like the inside of a tornado. Sometimes I hear Becks' voice calling my name. Then there's a man's voice. Gradually, the buffeting inside this whirlwind gets calmer. Now I begin to think I really can hear voices. Becks' tears are falling on my face. 'Joe, for God's sake…'

And there's a voice that I've not heard for so many years. 'Joe! You HAVE to wake up! This is absolutely non-negotiable!'

Slowly, not quite believing what I might see, not quite knowing if I'm hallucinating, I open my eyes. 'Dad?'

The smiling blue eyes of my father survey me appraisingly. 'You've grown.'

'What kept you?'

—ᴍ—

Things continue to improve rapidly after that. The squall is subsiding so we're not being chucked around like we were. Tommaso finds some morphine in Black Dog's first aid kit and that has the interesting side effect of making me slightly more gaga than usual. Lenny removes his bloodied T-shirt from my leg and wraps bandages round instead. 'Give it me, Lenny, I'll take it home for Mum to wash.' And half way through this morphine-induced nonsense I think… Mum. How are we going to prepare her for this?

Becks? She just sits quietly next to me, holding my hand as I lie there on the floor. Once, I ask her, 'You OK, Becks?' For an answer, she gives me a very long, gentle hug, her red hair falling over my face. Then we both go quiet, each feeling an insane gratitude for the other's being alive.

Dad comes back down the steps from the control room. It's only then that I notice that his black jeans and shirt are soaking wet. 'You been taking a dip, Dad?'

He nods solemnly. 'Salt water is excellent for the constitution, son. Now,' his voice becomes businesslike, 'We're to be paid a visit by two copters. The first to arrive will be an air ambulance which will take you to Fort William hospital.'

'Hospital? But I don't need...'

'No arguments. You were lucky that the bullet didn't lodge in your leg but this is not the Wild West, Joe.'

Becks gives my wrist a slight twist. 'You're going, Joe, so just shut up!'

Dad smiles. 'The second copter will remove our mutual friend and company to face summary justice, which the Scots are exceptionally good at.'

'Where is he?'

'Cuffed, gagged and blindfolded in a place where the sun don't shine and it smells quite foul. I locked him in the bilges.'

Becks grins. 'Good!'

Tommaso calls down, 'We are going to sort out Aquila's men and then take back Isla's RIB – OK, Joe?'

'Give them my love.'

Dad sits down on the floor next to me and Becks. I notice the single handcuff on his left wrist and some of the skin on his arm burned red and raw. 'You have quite a team, don't you Joe?'

'The best there is, Dad.'

'And you two have known each other for a long time, haven't you?'

Becks puts her other hand on mine. 'I can't remember a time when I didn't know Joe. But he can be a complete idiot.'

The radio in the control room above starts to squawk and Dad gets up to answer it. As he reaches the steps, he pauses and looks back. 'You're a lucky man, Joe.'

'I know.'

CHAPTER 14

Sebastian

The twin rotors of the big Sea King helicopter thunder like they're blowing the sky apart, as slowly I'm winched off the deck and upwards through the air. Remembering our rescue off the Avon Gorge, I make sure not to look down. The copter gets even louder as I go higher. I wonder if air ambulance paramedics suffer from poor hearing.

'You're nearly there, mate!' shouts a cheerful voice. Then they pull me inside and clip me onto a stretcher while the lift goes back down for Becks. She arrives looking a lot more composed than I feel. We look down at Dad as he waves from the deck. Becks waves back. 'Cheer up, Joe. He'll come to the hospital as soon as he's sorted out all the bad men.'

'You need to fasten your seatbelt, young lady.' The paramedic looks a bit like Brad Pitt, only younger.

'Oh, right.' She clips it on and with a surge of power, the copter heads for the shore. 'How's your leg?'

'Sore. Why did he have to shoot me in the leg, anyway?'

'God, Joe, the morphine's really got to you, hasn't it? Your leg was the only part of you he could shoot at from where he was – you've been incredibly lucky!'

'But… what was the second shot? I thought he'd hit you… '

'Your dad shot the gun out of his hand.'

'OK…'

'Then they had this fight. It was horrible with you bleeding so badly and we couldn't do anything. But your dad finished it quickly with a huge punch that knocked Aquila out.'

I look down at the white-tipped waves. The stealth ship and Black Dog have disappeared from view. But as soon as my heavy eyes close, I'm in the water beneath those huge hulls and some beast has its teeth clamped on my leg and is dragging me under.

—⁓—

When I wake up, I'm lying on a hospital bed with my right jean cut to the thigh and a thick bandage on my lower leg, which throbs like someone's applying rhythmic hammer blows. Becks is sitting next to me, munching hungrily on a bacon and egg sandwich. On the cupboard next to her is a glass of milk. 'Where did you get that?'

'They gave it me. There's one here for you.' She fishes in the cupboard and produces another egg and bacon and a bottle of water. 'They did an X-ray and said you didn't need an operation and there's no infection, so you can eat.'

'I slept through all that?'

'You were dead to the world. Well, the last time we slept was two days ago and you've had all that morphine as well…'

I heave myself up and unwrap the sandwich. 'Did they say when I can get out of here?'

'As soon as your dad comes.'

—⁊⁊—

Two hours later, a smiling nurse brings us tea; burger, peas and mashed potato, followed by ice cream. Evening is drawing in when biscuits and cups of tea arrive and we're now doing really well in the eating department.

When Dad arrives he's not alone. All our mates come crowding in with him. While Dad goes off to talk to the medics, Arnaud tuts disapprovingly, 'Just look at him! Sitting here stuffing himself while we run around taking back RIBs, taking down smelly tents…'

'Have you not had anything?'

Tommaso smiles, 'He's winding you up, Joe. As soon as we'd taken back the RIB, your dad bought us all fish and chips.'

'I guess Isla wasn't too happy about us borrowing her boat…'

'When we told her what Black Dog was really up to instead of fishing, she said she was glad to have helped.'

'That's one nice lady.'

Becks says, 'We'll write to her and thank her – no, better still, let's send her flowers!'

'Flowers are on their way.' Dad has come in quietly. 'And so do we all need to be. Arnaud – I have spoken to your father. He has sent a flight plan to your phone and to the helicopter management system.'

Arnaud holds out his hand. 'Thank you, Commander Grayling.'

Dad takes the hand firmly. 'Your father has always been my dearest friend, Arnaud. It is a great privilege to meet his son, especially in such circumstances. You will be taking Michel and Lenny, dropping off at Staverton for Lenny?'

'If that's OK with you, Lenny?'

Lenny's boxer face smiles. 'Sure – my car is there.'

'Lenny, Michel,' Dad shakes with them. 'I am so grateful to you all.'

He turns to Tommaso, who is almost unseen behind the other, bigger lads. 'And Tommaso....' Slowly, Tommaso approaches my father. Dad lays a hand on each of the boy's thin shoulders and looks at him with kind blue eyes. 'Christian tells me that, without you, this mission would not have been possible.' We all whoop agreement and two young nurses look around in alarm. 'The thanks I owe you are immeasurable, Tommaso. I would be very grateful if you would travel with me and Joe and Becks and stay with our family for a while. There's a great deal to talk about, isn't there?'

Tommaso holds out a hand that shakes very slightly. Before the tired boy can stagger, Dad takes his brother's son into his arms.

—◊—

The medics kit me out with crutches which everyone rags me about. Then Dad drives us all to the Fort William heliport in the battered Range Rover. 'Don't the police want this, Dad?'

'I've arranged to hand it over at the heliport. Forensically it's not hugely helpful, as you people have rather left your mark on it.'

'Right.'

He flicks a quick look at me. 'It's not a problem, Joe. There's enough evidence to put Aquila away for life, even before they bring in the munitions ship.'

'When's that going to happen?'

'The Scottish police have talked with the Royal Navy. The plan is to tow the stealth ship a good distance out into the Atlantic and undertake a detailed survey. There are concerns that there could be instabilities in the nuclear reactor.'

Becks asks, 'Instabilities?'

Dad shifts into gear as the traffic lights go green. 'The likes of Aquila are not particularly hot on maintenance of their boats and that can become a big problem with nuclear reactors. It could mean a leak of nuclear fuel, overheating...'

'Could it actually explode?'

'In an extreme situation, yes. But that's why the

190

Navy are taking what they call 'sensible precautions'. They know what they're doing – all our subs are nuclear powered.'

—⁓—

Night has fallen by the time we reach the heliport. Climbing out stiffly, I grab my crutches and we make our farewells to Arnaud, Michel and Lenny. 'Come to my gym for physio, Joe. Soon sort that leg.'

'Cheers, bud. I'll do that. And thanks for… everything.' We slap a high five and Lenny swings into the black copter.

Arnaud hugs Tommaso. 'Mon frère! I will take great care of Talia until you come to see us very soon!'

Tommaso looks at him steadily. 'Give her my love. I know she is very happy with you, my brother.'

Arnaud and I exchange a bear hug. 'When are you going to teach me to fly this copter, Arnaud?'

'As soon as you are off those crutches! I hope that will motivate you, my dear friend.' He climbs into the copter and a few seconds later, the rotors roar. We watch, until they're just a twinkling speck, far away in the night sky.

'The car is this way.'

I creak after Dad on my crutches, Becks giggling and Tommaso shepherding me solicitously. 'What car?'

'Christian has been most helpful, as usual.'

Immaculate coachwork gleaming gold, no sign

of the scars I inflicted on it, my first Bentley waits for us in the heliport car park. 'Precious!'

Dad looks at me quizzically. 'Christian did say it could have certain associations for you, Joe.'

—∞—

As soon as we leave Fort William, Becks and Tommaso fall into an exhausted sleep in the back seat. With hours of credit in my sleep bank, I've never felt so wide awake. For a while, I just watch Dad's hands on the steering wheel and gearshift, trying to get used to the fact that he really is here next to me. Then I think about what's going to happen when we arrive home.

'Dad, about Mum...'

'I know. She has always been on my mind, and most of all now.'

'It's going to be such a shock...'

'When I made contact with Christian, the first thing he offered to do was to prepare your mother. He will be phoning her... and he will know exactly what to say.'

'Monsieur was incredibly kind to us when we thought...'

Dad looks for a very long moment at the headlights streaming towards us. 'That's the part of this whole awful business that I feel worst about. That I put my family through such a dreadful ordeal, and after all those years of silence, is something I can never forgive myself for.'

'Wait up, Dad – surely you didn't even know what had happened at first?'

'I found out from Le Loup. The tragedy was that the truth had to be suppressed. It was only because Aquila and certain other parties thought I was dead that I managed to catch up with him on that mountain above Rome.'

'And then you found out who his hostages were.'

'The moment I saw Tommaso, I guessed he was Seb's son and that the daughter was being held as well. The only way through was a deal.'

'Which put you right where you didn't want to be. How did you escape from the stealth ship?'

'People are often careless about what they leave lying around. Oxyacetylene torches, for example.'

'And you burned your arm…?'

Dad flicks me a quick sideways look, his face suddenly serious. 'I noticed you've suffered some battle damage in the same area…'

My face feels hot. 'Please don't tell Mum. That was then.'

His hand gently touches my wrist with all the scabs and scars that I never want Mum or Becks to see. 'There's a lot that I have to be very sorry for, Joe.'

'Never mind that, Dad. How much time did you have to spend in that freezing water?'

'Less time than I expected. Your RIB was a total surprise. And of course it put a completely different complexion on things.'

'Well, we did manage to provide a few diversions.'

'Made my job a lot easier.' His voice goes very quiet. 'And in fact, although your getting shot is the last thing I'd ever have wanted, you saved my life, Joe.'

'How's that?'

'I'd immobilised the guy at the wheel but if you hadn't distracted our mutual friend as I climbed on deck, the bullet that got your leg would have been aimed at my head.'

I'm silent, thinking how horribly close we came to losing Dad forever, just when we believed we had him back. 'Seb – was that your brother's name?'

He pauses while we overtake a convoy of artics. 'Sebastian and I weren't so much brothers as best mates. Right through our childhoods and into our teens and twenties. Although he was two years older than me, we looked very alike; it was almost the incredibly close relationship that twins have.'

'Like Tommaso and Talia? Even though he'd never met his sister, he'd loved her ever since he found out she existed.'

He nods. 'Seb and I both went to Oxford, then we were brothers in arms in the SAS for several scorching years. After that, we both went into the totally secretive arm of MI6 that's known only as the network.'

'When did it all go wrong with Seb, Dad?' We're on really bendy roads now and I can feel from my popping ears that we're gradually making the descent from the Highlands. I can smell the salt water from Dad's sea-soaked clothes.

194

'Seb was working undercover as a chauffeur and bodyguard for the Contessa. He'd only been there for a few months when he went into radio silence. It was a long time after when we got the news. He'd turned; gone to work for her. But I only found out far more recently that he'd fallen in love with her.'

'And so... he became the black sheep? No one ever got told...?'

'I had not long been married to your mother. I had just started to work with Christian in the network. Joe, I would not have known how to begin to tell them about Seb.'

'It didn't last long, did it? After the twins were born?'

'No. Because by then, the viper had set her sights on Christian, who had dared to be in love with another woman...'

'Monsieur told us she murdered his wife.'

'Which made it all the more impossible to tell anyone. And I'm afraid it made Seb all the more tainted by association.'

'And then, years later, you were working for her undercover as a chauffeur and bodyguard...'

'The irony wasn't lost on me, Joe.'

'Did she know you were Uncle Seb's brother?'

'Oh yes. But I'd created a cast-iron cover from my work with other hell's angels ..'

'Like the Black Knight?'

'Correct. You've been meticulous with the ruby stick.'

'And was Uncle Seb watching you, as Michelangelo, all that time?'

'He must have been. But although things began to go wrong in the network – there were ambushes, kidnappings, all of which seemed to have an insider involved – he never betrayed me. And then, when he discovered that I'd had to leave without knowing that you were practically knocking at death's door, he made this extraordinary… sacrifice, is the only word.'

'He impersonated you…?'

'Right down to making sure that he had my family photos and the ruby memory stick on him. If he hadn't passed himself off as me, I wouldn't be here now. Instead… we've lost him…'

'Did you always keep on loving your brother, Dad?

Dad stares at the road ahead, with just the odd pair of headlights coming towards us now. 'It was like an amputation, losing Seb. Before I found out everything, I was very angry with him.'

'Tommaso said it helped him to love his dad again, when he discovered how he died, what he did…?'

'Tommaso can teach me a thing or two.' Dad glances in the rear view mirror as Tommaso stirs and Becks covers a yawn. 'I can feel a break coming on, can't you?'

We're at a motorway services near Carlisle as Dad swings Precious into the car park. Becks glances in the door mirror. 'Oh God, I was dreaming my hair looked like this – and it does!'

Tommaso looks all in. I creak alongside him. 'You OK, bud?'

He smiles wearily, 'I think it is just the relief, Joe.'

After burgers and coffee, we head back on down the motorway. Dad glances at me. 'So what's with this Precious, then?'

'It's a very long story, Dad.'

'It's a very long drive, Joe.'

My mobile goes. 'It's Mum.'

Dad says, 'Put it into the hands free.'

So we all hear Mum's voice, as tight as a wire. 'Your grandad's been admitted to hospital with chest pains, Joe. Can you come straight to Gloucester Royal?'

CHAPTER 15

Homecoming

As the Bentley approaches the Gloucester exit, Dad flicks a glance backwards. 'Are you OK with going straight to the hospital, Becks? Only...'

She says quietly, 'I love Joe's grandad... he's the sweetest man...'

Dad swings onto the slip road. 'It could be a very good thing for Nina's father to see you all, if he is well enough.'

Dawn is breaking with grey skies and drizzling rain as we park at Gloucester Royal. The four of us crowd into the lift and I shuffle so as not to trip people over with my crutches. I remember the last time I could smell this mix of disinfectant and cooked food. Not in the place where Monsieur was cared for; that carries memories of latte, pastries, bright bullets and learning that Dad was alive. No, this smell comes back to me from the hospital in Paris where Monsieur waited for me, to tell me that Dad was dead. And... this man standing beside me now, the smell of sea water on his clothes... The lift jolts to a halt on the third floor and I stagger as a crutch slips. Instantly, Dad's hand is beneath my elbow.

In the A & E waiting room there's a dude in a wheelchair with a leg in a bloodied bandage, muttering to himself like he could explode any moment; he's the only one there. Dad steers us all into chairs well away from the mutterer. 'I'll check at Reception.'

Just as he says that, twin blue doors opposite with a sign saying 'Wards' swing open and Mum comes through with her brisk walk. Her dark hair looks like the usual hurricane has been through it, and weirdly, she's dressed just like Dad, in a black top and jeans; except she's wearing boots not trainers. She looks even thinner than when I last saw her. For what seems minutes, but can only be a second, she stops and stands completely still, staring at Dad like he's some kind of dream. Then he moves swiftly forward and wraps his arms round her so that I can't see her at all. I hear him whisper, 'It's over, Nina. How's your Dad?'

—∽∾—

With more colour in her face than I've seen for a long time, Mum sips a coffee from the machine. Dad sits next to her and never takes his eyes from her face. She speaks slowly, like someone who's coming round from a nightmare. 'They're… doing tests, now. He's on a defibrillator, in case…'

'Perfectly normal procedure, you know that, love.'

'But it was just such a shock....'

Dad puts an arm round her. 'After all those years when he was so strong for you... of course it was a shock.'

Mum looks round at me and Becks and then sees another pair of eyes gazing at her and Dad with extreme concern. 'I do apologise, my dear... you must be Tommaso. Christian told me...'

He comes to her, hand outstretched in his courteous way. 'I am so sorry about Joe's grandad, Mrs Grayling.'

'Oh, my dear, Aunt Nina, please!' Mum jumps up and hugs him gently, 'He's your family now, Tommaso – and we owe you so much!' She turns to Becks, 'And you, you extraordinary girl, for putting up with this wayward son of ours!'

Becks gives Mum a hug. 'He's had to put up with a lot of nagging from me, don't you worry! Have they said how long the tests will take?'

'It could be a while, I'm afraid.'

I grab a straying crutch as it tries to ambush an innocent passer-by. 'Then we'll wait it out, Mum.'

— ⁊⁊ —

During the three and a half hour wait, Mum and Dad talk in low tones and never stop holding hands. Becks and Tommaso doze off in their chairs. I'm at the machine, juggling crutches and fifty pence pieces to get us some drinks, when a grey-haired consultant comes in. 'Mrs St Aubin?'

Mum gets up, Dad's arm round her. 'Your father has responded well to the treatment, Mrs St Aubin. But there will need to be an intervention; if you would come this way…?'

I hand out fizzy Highland Spring to Becks and Tommaso. 'What's an intervention?'

There's a hiss as Becks opens her drink. 'I think it's an operation.'

—⁂—

The grey morning has turned into continuously lashing rain that bashes on the windows of the waiting room. Every available chair is occupied with mums and crying children, but thankfully the muttering guy with the messy bandage and worse language has gone. When Mum and Dad come back, Dad nods to me, 'You can all go in and see your grandad, Joe… just don't offer to take him clubbing quite yet, OK?'

Grandad is sitting up in bed with a drip going into his arm and some pads on wires taped to his chest beneath a white gown. Without his glasses, he looks younger and more frail but he beams as we come quietly in. 'Joe, you young rascal! What on earth have you been up to now?'

I give him a careful hug. 'You know me, Grandad. Always getting into trouble.'

'And Becks, my dear girl, I'm so glad to see you back in one piece. I daresay you were his minder, most of the time?'

She gives him a kiss on his forehead. 'When he's ready, ask him about the tent!'

Grandad looks at Tommaso, who stands shyly behind us. 'Tommaso, it gives me such joy to meet you at last!' He holds out his hands; Tommaso comes forward and slips his young hands into Grandad's wrinkled ones. 'I am so terribly sorry about your brave father. But you will always be cherished by his family.' Eyes bright, Tommaso smiles and nods his thanks.

Silently, Dad has entered the room. He wraps an arm round Tommaso's thin shoulders and looks at Grandad. 'I think we call it a day, Dad, don't you? Until tomorrow?'

'You have all done me more good than you can imagine.' Grandad's bright smile follows us out of the door.

Back in the waiting room, we sit down with Mum as Dad explains. 'Your mum's father needs a very specialised heart operation, hopefully within the next few days.'

'Is he going to be alright?'

'The consultant says he should make a full recovery.'

'You can crash in my room tonight, Bro. We've got this lilo.'

Tommaso grins. 'Has to be better than that tent!'

—∽—

When we get to Becks' house, Steve is bending

over the engine bay of his battered Ford Ka. He straightens up and stares at Precious for the second time. 'Blimey, sis. Have you won the lottery and bought it?'

She gives me a quick hug, 'There's all that stuff of ours at the chateau, isn't there?'

Dad says, 'No problem, Becks. Christian will send it on.' He gets out and opens the car door for her, with the same old-fashioned gallantry that Grandad has.

'Thanks, Mr Grayling.'

'The thanks are all from me, Becks. I wouldn't be here if it wasn't for you and the team.'

While Dad slides discreetly back into the driver's seat and talks to Mum, I give Becks a long hug. 'You going into school tomorrow?'

'Course I am. I'm so predictable. And why don't you come, just to check out re-sits?

'I… I'm not sure, Becks…'

'That's alright.' She takes my face between her hands. 'Just be kind to yourself, OK? Promise?'

'Promise. Oh, by the way, Becks?'

About to go in, she pauses and turns. 'Yeah?'

'Predictable is one of the things you are not.'

She blows me a kiss. 'I'll work on it then.'

'Don't try too hard.'

—w—

The Bentley pulls up with a quiet purr outside our house. Jack's window is open; he's playing his sax to

203

a backing track. Despite the volume he must have ears like radar, because the front door opens before we get to it. And suddenly, Jack and Dad are face to face. Jack's blond hair is in aggressive hedgehog mode, he's in the most ripped jeans and top I've ever seen and he's got taller. We all stop dead, at a loss for words; but Jack knows what to say. 'How's Grandad?'

Dad says, 'It's good news, Jack. Shall we talk about it? If you remember me at all?'

Jack grabs Dad's hand and tows him towards the stairs. 'I remember your voice, Dad. Would you like to see my fish?'

Mum goes to sit down in the lounge, looking completely drained and elated at the same time. I make her a coffee and glance at my watch. 'How about Tommaso and I nip out for burger and chips?'

'That would be lovely, Joe. You're rather brilliant on those crutches.' Her head falls back onto the armchair.

'You've been up all night, haven't you Mum? Why don't you grab some sleep?'

'I might just do that…'

Tommaso comes with me as I creak upstairs on my crutches and he grabs the duvet off my bed. We wrap Mum up cosily; she's fast asleep, her coffee untouched. It can't be very often that you nearly lose your father and get your long-lost husband back in the same night.

Tommaso seems preoccupied as we head down the street to MacDonald's. On the pavement, two crows are pecking at some chips. 'What's on your mind, bud?'

'I was thinking… of when I told Talia how our father died. And she told me about our mother.'

'Yeah?'

'Talia said she could not love our mother because she never felt loved by her. She feels bad about that now.'

I stop. 'She shouldn't, Tommaso.'

'Our mother killed Monsieur's wife, didn't she?'

'Yes…'

'And yet he still tried to save her life? Arnaud told me.'

'He said to me that leaving her to drown without trying to save her wouldn't have brought his wife back.'

'So… he must have forgiven her?'

'I guess he had.'

'I think that if Talia could forgive our mother for not loving her, she would feel better?'

'I've come to realise that Monsieur is a very wise man, Tommaso. And so are you.'

When we get back, Tommaso carrying bags of Big Macs and Cokes, we pause outside the front door.

The soulful sound of 'Misty' drifts through Jack's open window. Tommaso smiles that thin smile. 'I would love to learn the saxophone.'

'Jack would love it if you did! He wants to set up his own jazz band.'

When we go in, Dad comes down the stairs. 'You stars!' He peeps in on Mum, who is still sleeping soundly in the lounge, grabs Big Macs and Cokes for Jack and himself, and bounds back upstairs. Jack's jazz serenade of his new dad continues.

Tommaso and I go into the kitchen to munch our burgers. As soon as we sit down, Fats bursts through the cat flap and pushes his big, chunky body against my legs. 'Fats! I might've known you'd show up at the first sign of food.' I pass him a chip; he looks at it with disdain, and carefully sniffs around Tommaso's trainers. 'D'you think he can smell Corbo?'

'More likely the fish and chips your dad bought us.'

'I bet Corbo will be waiting for you at the chateau.'

'He is very independent... but it would be good.'

I take a large bite of burger and chomp slowly. 'Will you go to live there, Tommaso? I mean, Monsieur has become Talia's guardian...?'

He leans down to stroke Fats. 'It is difficult, Joe. I have found my sister but I have also found family here who are dear to me...'

I pick up Fats, who seems to have got heavier. With a protesting miaow, he jumps off my lap and goes back to investigating Tommaso's trainers. 'Let's not worry about it tonight. Main thing is, we're all in one piece, more or less. And I've got you to thank for that, bro.'

'Shall we see if your mother has woken?'

As we head for the lounge, Dad and Jack come down the stairs. Dad whispers, 'I'll make sure your mum gets something to eat.'

'Cool. Jack, can we see your fish? How's the Black Ghost?'

'Don't see much of him but he's still alive.'

'Tommaso would love to learn sax. Could we er…?'

Jack's face lights up for the second time today. 'Oh, amazing! Like, tenor, alto or what?'

'You play alto, yes?'

'Yep, that's my usual.'

'I love the sound of tenor.'

'You love tenor… walk this way, Tommaso. Oh, and you can come too, Joe'

'You're too kind, Jack.' Creakingly, I follow them up to Jack's room.

Hours later, jazz ringing in my ears, I remember where the lilo is, dig it out of the wardrobe and find Tommaso a sleeping bag and a spare toothbrush. Fats is right where my feet normally are. Tommaso strokes the sleek fur and then curls up in his sleeping bag, his eyes closing as his head hits the pillow. My eyes close with Fats' deep rumbles, as he pads up to my pillow and purrs loudly in my right ear.

The following afternoon, Tommaso and I are chilling out with a movie and pizza and Mum is with Dad in the hospital, when Dad calls. 'It was a long operation, but he's come through like a champ. There'll be regular checkups, of course…'

'Can we come and see him?'

'He's still getting over the anaesthetic. I'll take you both in tomorrow.'

—ɯ—

Three days later, Dad brings me and Tommaso tea in bed earlier than usual. He's dressed in the grey suit that I borrowed for my job interview with Monsieur. He says gently, 'We have some respects to pay, Tommaso. Joe will sort you both out with two of my suits.'

Outside the small country churchyard, the Bentley's engine whispers into silence. Someone has cut the grass between the gravestones and the air is full of the fresh, green smell. Dad takes the wreath out of the boot and with his arm round Tommaso, leads the way through the wooden gate with its tiled archway. Some tiny, delicate mosses are growing on the wood; I reach out to touch one as we pass. Mum whispers, 'Lichens. They only grow where the air is very pure.'

The new gravestone, in its dark granite, is engraved with the words, 'Sebastian John Grayling. Beloved father and brother.'

'May I, Uncle?'

'Of course.' Dad hands the wreath to Tommaso. Its myriads of small, dark green leaves have a strong scent. Tommaso kneels and lays it on the stone, pausing for a moment in deep thought. Then he gets up, his face with some of that old pallor and weariness.

'Come, my dear.' With a gentle arm around Tommaso, Mum walks with him back to the car.

Dad remains, gazing at the simple tablet. 'He was a far better man than I am, Joe.'

'How's that, Dad?'

'The real reason why I never told people about Seb was that I couldn't forgive him.'

'And have you now?'

'Dear God, yes, Joe. After what he did...'

'So now it's just yourself, isn't it?'

'Sorry?'

'You have to forgive yourself, Dad. And you can – after what you did for Talia and Tommaso.' With a last glance back at the peaceful gravestone, I slip my hand into his.

—⚏—

That evening, Mum and Dad ask Jack to come and have a quiet chat with them and I hope he's not in trouble. Tommaso is practising with Jack's sax in his room when Monsieur calls me on Skype. His grey eyes are more intense than usual.

'Is... is something wrong, Monsieur?'

'Not at all, Joe. I… have a proposition to put to you. It goes without saying that I have already discussed it with your mother and father.'

'You're being very mysterious, Monsieur.'

'It's very simple, really. In this chateau that has been my family's home from generation to generation, there are many rooms and apartments. For years, it has been a lonely place. It would be a joy if your family and Becks would like to come and live here with us, Joe.'

I stare at the screen, wondering if I've heard right. 'You mean, for good? Not just a holiday?'

'For as long as you wish.'

'And Arnaud, Talia and Tommaso will all be there?'

'It gives Tommaso the chance to be with all the people he loves. I called him earlier this evening.'

'Can Grandad come?'

'As soon as he is fully recovered, your father will bring him.'

'What does Jack think of it?'

'Your parents are talking to him now. There is an excellent jazz scene in Aix which, your mother thinks, will strongly influence his decision. And she knows the college well.'

'Can I go and ask Becks?'

He nods. 'I felt it should come from you.'

'We'll call you… we won't be long, Monsieur.'

'You must take your time, Joe. It is a very big decision.'

When I get to Becks' house, completely out of

breath on my creaky crutches, her light is the only one that's on. I ring the doorbell; she looks warily out of her window and her eyes widen. Opening the door, she says, 'This is a funny time to come for a hobble round here, isn't it?'

'No.' We go into the lounge, where we can't sit down because most of the furniture is covered with bits of Steve's motorbike on newspapers; it stinks of engine oil. 'Becks, you know how much we both love Monsieur's place?'

'Course I do. I hate coming home after being there.'

'How would you like to live there with all of us, and never have to come back here again?'

She frowns. 'You're not joking, are you? No, you wouldn't joke about something like this.'

'You need to be sure, Becks. I mean, you might miss your mates back at school?'

'All my best mates would be there, Joe. Except for Lenny, and he can visit, can't he? And we can go back and see him.'

'Monsieur says there's a good college, so you won't miss out on school.'

Her green eyes sparkle. 'You might even join me there!'

'Yeah, I might, too. So…?'

She looks thoughtful. 'So… I was just wondering what it's like to kiss a guy on crutches…?'

'First time for everything…'

—∞—

Things move very quickly the next day. Dad books a removal lorry to take our stuff, and Jack and I pack, helped by Tommaso. Mum's put out a suitcase and I throw my clothes into it. I check in the back of the wardrobe; and there, all crumpled, is the chauffeur's uniform that marked the start of my brilliant career.

'I didn't know if you'd want to keep it.' Mum is standing in the doorway with Dad.

'You have some tales to tell me, don't you Joe?' Dad's face is serious but his eyes are smiling.

'All done.' Tommaso drags Jack's case onto the landing.

I retrieve the jacket and trousers, fold them and pack them in my case. 'You never know. Right, I'm off to Becks' to give her a hand.'

Dad hands me my crutches. 'I'll give you a lift.'

At Becks' place, the front door is open. Helping me out, Dad says quietly, 'I think it's best if you handle this, Joe.'

Steve calls from upstairs, 'Come on up, mate! Becks has popped into school to say her goodbyes.' He's in Becks' room, throwing her clothes into a battered suitcase. 'What have you done to your leg?'

'Fell over. I'll pack Becks' stuff, Steve. I expect you've got things to do.'

He straightens up and I can smell an unwashed body and stale beer. 'As a matter of fact, I 'ave got more important things to do than pack for my sister.'

Taking a deep breath, I start folding Becks' clothes carefully and laying them in the suitcase.

'I mean, why would she want to leave home anyway?'

I check in the drawers, stunned by how few clothes and belongings Becks has. A pink teddy tumbles out of the wardrobe; it's the one she used to try and set me free from Bertolini. I tuck it into the suitcase. 'She'd rather live in France, that's all.'

'She can't just bunk off like that.'

I take Becks' winter coat out of the wardrobe. 'She can, actually. She's over sixteen. She can live wherever she chooses.'

'What about school?'

'There's a good college in Aix.' At the back of the wardrobe is a pile of hardback novels; perhaps these were what made Becks' case so heavy on the way to Paris. One of them is 'Treasure Island' by Robert Louis Stevenson. I scoop them all up.

'Oh, nice. And you're all living in some kind of mansion...'

'Something like that.'

'Shame I'm not seeing Annette anymore. We could pay you a visit...'

I snap shut the locks on the suitcase and pick it up. 'Yeah, shame isn't it? I've left the school uniform – sure you can flog it. Bye, Steve.' And with that, I make my precarious way back down the stairs sliding the case at my side, and limp out of the door. Dad opens the boot, I load up Becks' suitcase and we drive off without a backwards glance.

That night, I call her. 'I packed your pink teddy.'

'Oh sweet! What time tomorrow morning?'

'Really early, like 5.15?'
'I can't wait!'

—m—

When we get to Becks' place, there are no lights on at all. She stands shivering on the pavement in her thin jacket. I get out and slide her in between me and Jack, while Tommaso smiles at her from the front passenger seat. As soon as Becks is belted, Dad accelerates away, heading for the M5 and Southampton ferry port.

'Where's your mum, Joe?'

Even in the dim light, I can see the dark shadows under Becks' eyes. 'She's coming tomorrow – stuff to do with selling the house. Steve not at home?'

'Staying at his new girlfriend's place, I expect.'

'And your dad?'

'Oh… I don't know where he is right now.' She covers a huge yawn.

'You didn't get much sleep, did you?'

'The people next door like to party on a Friday night.'

'You've got a pillow here.' I put my arm round her so that she can rest her head on my shoulder. Becks sleeps all the way to the ferry port. Sometimes I stroke her hair. It's incredibly soft and floaty and twice I get a slight electric shock from it. I can't remember much about the ferry, so we must both have slept all the way across the Channel.

A few miles before the turn to the chateau, Arnaud calls and Dad switches him onto the hands-free. 'We're doing an extreme barbecue. Orders, please!' He reels off a vast menu.

'I can't remember the stuff at the beginning... can you text it?'

He sighs. 'Just state preferences – surf, turf or vegetarian?'

'You know I'm a meat man, Arnaud. What about you, Jack?'

'Oh, meat please.'

'Becks, what sort of food mood are you in?

'What's Talia having?'

'Tuna and swordfish.'

'I'm in with that.'

'That makes it easy. Ciao!'

'I bet you've already put your order in, Dad?'

'Fraid so, Joe. You have a very opportunistic father.'

'Guess you need that instinct to stay alive...'

In the rear view mirror, his blue eyes sparkle with me in his sights. 'You should know, son. You've done a pretty good job of that yourself, thank God.'

Jack stares as Dad drives the Bentley up to the tall, cast-iron gates of L'Étoile and they swing silently open. The Provençale sun blazes down onto the sparkling fountains with their curvy statues. Above us rises the chateau, its centuries old stone mellow in the sunlight. Dad jumps out of the car, opens the boot and takes Jack's sax. 'Let's go to the party, shall we?' He wraps an arm around Jack's shoulders and they swing away down the tree walk where Becks and I first heard Corbo on that strange, moonlit night.

Tommaso hands me my crutches. 'How is your leg after the journey, Joe?'

'Not bad at all.'

On the way through the tree walk, Becks stops to look at a fountain that tumbles down a wall of grey pebbles into a pond full of lily pads. 'I love this place.'

Dad calls, 'Come on you lot – or all the food will be gone!'

Becks breaks into a run. 'Race you!'

'That is so not fair!' I try a kind of jungle swing on the crutches.

'Relax, Joe.' Tommaso puts a hand on my arm as Becks disappears into the trees. 'We are in no hurry right now.'

We emerge from the tree walk and take in the view. Madame de L'Étang and Talia are preparing green salads on a trestle table. Closely observed by Dad and Jack, Arnaud is presiding over a barbeque loaded with steaks and fish. Through the open glass doors of the lounge drift the languid chords of Pink Floyd's 'Wish you were here'. And Monsieur is coming forward to greet Becks, who's kicking off her shoes and snuggling her toes into the soft grass. He hugs her and I notice he's got rid of the sling. 'My dear Becks, we're so happy that you could be with us all.'

'I wouldn't want to be anywhere else!' As she smiles back at Monsieur, Becks' fiery hair is glowing in the sun. I stare, like it's the first time I've ever seen her.

Monsieur turns to me and holds out his hand. 'My congratulations, Joe, on your extraordinary mission.'

'It was Tommaso who was the real leader, Monsieur.'

'You have all proved yourselves in a quite remarkable way.'

Arnaud calls, 'It is time for the toast!'

Everyone cheers and Dad pops a cork for bubbly all round. I raise my glass. 'To Grandad!'

'To Grandad!'

Arnaud solemnly proclaims, 'To us!'

Amid the shouting and laughter there's a raucous note that wasn't there just now. With a storm of dark wings, Corbo settles on Tommaso's shoulder. He smiles. 'To each and every one of us.'

CHAPTER 16

Mistral

At L'Étoile, we all get to choose our rooms. Becks and I go for the ones we had before, with the rainbow windows and the balconies looking onto the garden. Jack, thankfully, opts for the basement, where he has an entire apartment to make a lot of noise that we won't hear. Arnaud already has his own apartment near his father's, on the first floor. Tommaso and Talia have balcony rooms on the third floor like us, looking out onto another part of the garden. Mum and Dad have an apartment on most of the second floor. Grandad's apartment is being set up on the ground floor to make it easy for him to get around.

On day two, Monsieur takes us all to the college in Aix and gets us enrolled for September. Just like that. Arnaud says, 'This college is a bit special – they have an exchange system which allows students from all over the world to study here.'

'Right. What *will* we be studying?'

'You choose when you start. Fast track French of course, for all four of you.'

Fats and Jack's fish arrive by pet carrier the next day. Fats is very grumpy about his change of territory, and Jack is kept busy settling his fish. Monsieur has bought a tenor sax for Tommaso, and he and Jack spend many hours in Jack's basement.

Three weeks later, Dad brings Grandad to L'Étoile. It's his eightieth birthday and Madame, Becks and Talia have been in the kitchen all morning. The result is a cake that's a miniature version of L'Étoile, with a candle for each of the chimneys and even a tiny sixteen point star on the front door. We all sit round the table in the dining room and Grandad blows out the eight candles, one by one. 'So I'm just a child, after all! I always knew it.'

Becks hugs him gently. 'You're amazing!'

Not long after, Grandad starts to look very tired. Dad helps him into the wheelchair. 'Can you get some water for your grandad, please, Joe? I'll see him into bed.'

'I'll do it.' Becks picks up Grandad's spectacle case and disappears into the kitchen.

—⚬⚬—

Later on that night, Becks and I are the last ones watching a horror movie after all the others have gone to bed, when Monsieur looks in. 'Could you join us for a minute or two please, Joe? Your father and I will be in the study.'

Becks stifles a yawn. 'Well, I'm off. See you tomorrow.'

As she makes her way upstairs, I go into the study with its wood panelled walls and mellow lighting. On a small desk is the photo of Dad and Monsieur at Courchevel that I gave Monsieur to copy. 'Sit down, Joe.' Monsieur takes my crutches as I lower myself into the armchair.

Dad is looking at an email on Monsieur's computer and exclaiming under his breath. 'I can hardly believe this.'

'What's happened?'

'The Navy put two frigates on the case but they let her slip.'

'What, the stealth ship? She's gone?'

'Ariadne is her name. And a fine spider's web she's spun for us all!'

'But, how?'

Monsieur sits down next to me. 'She was closely guarded, so it could only have been by remote control. Possibly from a helicopter.'

Dad frowns. 'But by whom? Aquila's army of mercenaries is in tatters without their leader.'

'Dad, we came across some quite close friends of your man with the hat. Like, people who seemed to be financing him?'

'Would you like to tell us about this, Joe?'

'I thought you must have known…'

'Never assume how much your elders know, Joe. Usually, it's a lot less than you do.'

When I describe the younger guest and the white-haired dude who could have been his father, Dad shows me a picture on his phone. 'Is this the older one?'

'I think so…'

He pulls up another photo. 'And the younger one?' Those brown eyes that looked so careless and dangerous stare right at me.

'Yeah, that's definitely him. Who is he?'

Dad says quietly, 'Gregorio Salvatore. His father is known simply as The Judge; presumably because few escape his death sentence if he doesn't like their face. You're looking at the moneymen who've been keeping Aquila afloat. They will have taken the Ariadne, God knows where, to try and recoup their loan.'

'Will they go to the fifth co-ordinate, where Stetson was headed?'

'They haven't the nerve or the idiocy to brave the Belgian Congo. No, my guess is, they'll hide the Ariadne in some unlikely place and then communicate with the illegal arms market.'

'So, there's nothing we can do?'

Monsieur says, 'We'll alert the network to the situation. But our time out there is over, Joe. Too much exposure puts other agents at risk.'

'So, are you guys, like, retired?'

Dad sits down on my other side. 'Not exactly. But we won't be out in the field.'

'So you're not going away again?'

'No – except that your mother and I intend to take a very long holiday together.'

'So what's this "not exactly"?'

'Christian and I can still help with communication and co-ordination; we have some experience between us both.'

'So you'll be running the show from here?'

'Yes. And that's all, Joe. A no-risk arena.'

Monsieur gets up and hands me my crutches. 'You have achieved your extraordinary mission, Joe. It is time for you to live an ordinary life again.'

I don't get up. 'Suppose that an ordinary life is not what I want, Monsieur?'

Dad's blue eyes look directly at me. 'What *do* you want, Joe? We're listening.'

'I've, like, felt useful doing what we've been doing. I wouldn't mind doing some more?'

Dad and Monsieur exchange glances. This suddenly feels like a job interview. Monsieur says softly, 'You would still need to go to the college, Joe.'

'D'accord, Monsieur.'

'And Becks? What does she want? She is extremely intelligent.'

'Only to be head of the most secret service on the planet. That's all Becks wants.'

Monsieur looks directly at me. 'You have seen the price that can be paid for an occupation like this, haven't you, Joe? Perhaps you need some time to think it over?'

I return his gaze. 'I've seen the price, Monsieur. When the time comes, I'll find out if I can pay it, won't I?'

Monsieur's face is grave. 'It may not be just you who pays the price, Joe. You have seen that, too, haven't you?'

Now I don't know what to say. Monsieur puts his hand gently on my arm. 'I still think that you need time for reflection, Joe. Just to put some distance between all that has passed and your future.'

'Christian's right, Joe. You've all shown yourselves to be hugely capable and ridiculously brave. But there are other roles that don't carry such a penalty.'

'I'll bet they're not as interesting. What does Arnaud think, Monsieur?'

'At the moment he is simply concerned for Talia.'

'Of course he is, Monsieur. And what about Tommaso? He's had enough – he and Talia need an ordinary life, don't they?'

'Have you talked to Tommaso about this, Joe?

'No, Monsieur. And I won't be doing it any time soon.'

'Quite right. Leave it up to him, Joe.'

—◊—

They put us all in the same class at the college, except for Jack, because he's younger. But he's cool; they've made him the leader of the college jazz band. We all get special French lessons; Talia and Tommaso are picking it up incredibly quickly. They say it's a lot closer to Italian than English is. Arnaud, Monsieur and Mum give us extra coaching at home. At meal times, French is what you speak. Dad jokes that he'd better join us at school to brush up his own French.

Most mornings, when I look out from my balcony and wave to Becks, Corbo sits on the railing, watching us. When Tommaso walks with us in the garden, the raven always rides on his shoulder.

But the hot summer days are almost over. Today, the air is cooler. The Mistral's high, moaning note intensifies as we go towards autumn. In my room, lit by its rainbow windows when the moon shines through, I dream of the stealth ship on these nights. With every gust that blows, I see the Ariadne's huge, crab-like form sliding across the waves into the dark.